DEAD AS A DODO

A WILDWOOD WITCH MYSTERY: BOOK 3

ELLE ADAMS

Being Head Witch had its perks, but compulsory magic lessons from my grandmother's ghost was definitely not one of them. Grandma's transparent figure hovered above the desk in the office—formerly hers, now mine—as she shouted out instructions and reprimands.

"You're slouching too much," she bellowed at me. "Hold the sceptre more upright."

"That's because I've been standing here for over an hour." My shoulder ached from the strain of holding the pointed instrument vertically in the air, since the sceptre was more than twice the length of a regular wand and required a lot more finesse to manoeuvre without accidentally hitting people in the face. Or hitting my*self* in the face, come to that. I tried to ignore my muscles' protest and straightened the sceptre so that it pointed upward. "Happy?"

"No," Grandma replied. "You're holding it as if it was a bomb, not a wand."

"That's because it pretty much is."

Bulkiness and awkwardness to wield aside, the sceptre amplified my magic far beyond my usual capabilities and was downright hazardous to anyone standing in its path. As far as I was concerned, that was reason enough to keep its use to a minimum, especially in a confined space.

"This isn't the best place to practise, you know."

While I'd considerably cleaned up some of the clutter in the back of the room with the aid of my brother and my assistant, Chloe, that didn't mean there weren't plenty of valuable items at potential risk of being hit by the sceptre's magic. Like the rows of filing cabinets filled with paperwork going back to before I was born, the cupboard full of rare potion ingredients, or the textbooks and other paraphernalia crammed onto the shelves that occupied all the remaining space. Except Chloe's desk, tucked beneath the window, where she sat typing away on her laptop and seemingly oblivious to the office's other occupants. I didn't think she'd appreciate being hit by a stray spell either though.

"If you want every witch in the building to see how little grasp you have on the sceptre's magic, then you're welcome to practise outside on the lawn instead," Grandma said caustically. "Or on the roof if you'd prefer."

I scowled at her. Aside from Grandma's well-honed knack for hitting on my sore spots having remained intact even beyond the grave, she knew as well as anyone that my problem wasn't a lack of skill but a lack of control over the giant nuclear weapon that I now had to carry everywhere with me. Casting a temporary stopping spell using the sceptre effectively turned a person into a life-sized statue for minutes or hours, while conjuring up a single leaf would run the risk of an entire forest crash-landing in my office. Besides, the sceptre wasn't to be used for trivial purposes, as Grandma herself had impressed upon me in our first lesson together.

Supposedly, I was meant to be grateful she'd deigned to give me lessons at all, as my grandmother had been by far the longest-serving Head Witch in the region and had been parted from the sceptre only upon her death. I rather hoped to avoid following in her footsteps, especially the last part, but the rules were clear: I was bound to wield the sceptre until the time came for it to choose someone else.

Or until someone murdered me for it, but I tried not to think too hard about that possibility.

Grandma's familiar, Carmilla, looked up from where she lay curled up on the windowsill, her mouth opening in a wide yawn. "Give it a rest. Nobody will be critiquing her posture until she meets the other Head Witches. Besides, so far, their schedules seem to be booked up."

I glanced over at the half-bald black cat, surprised that she'd stand up for me over her former owner, but she no doubt wanted to avoid a repeat of our last lesson, in which I'd accidentally levitated her into the air along with everything else in the office when casting a simple flight charm.

"So far," Grandma said ominously. "When that changes, you need to be prepared, Robin."

"I'm aware, but I doubt I'll have to actually use the sceptre *on* the other Head Witches."

Learning how to use my fancy new wand was just one of the many responsibilities of my new title, but as of yet, I hadn't been granted the dubious honour of meeting all the other Head Witches. A significant part of me was relieved to put off the task, since dealing with the coven leaders in Wildwood Heath alone had been quite enough on its own. I'd always been comfortable in knowing I didn't quite fit in among the stuck-up and inwardly focused witches who led the covens that had been entrenched in the region for generations, but the one truth that had kept me sane throughout my childhood had been the knowledge that they couldn't legally force me to stick around.

Magically though? The sceptre's power was binding, and I had no doubt the universe was laughing its tail off at me for thinking I'd escaped.

"You never know," said Grandma. "Be on your guard."

"Noted."

Honestly. Grandma herself had rarely used the sceptre when she'd held the title, but she'd had no problem with dealing with the seemingly endless reams of paperwork that also came as a side effect of the position. I was more or less the opposite, and it took a great deal of patience to ignore my grandmother's grumbling about me delegating such tasks to my assistant. Chloe was far better suited for filling out paperwork than I was, but as for wielding the sceptre… that part was entirely up to me. Which meant tolerating daily lessons from Grandma's ghost.

Fortunately, this one was at an end. A moment after the clock hit five thirty p.m., the door nudged inwards, and my red squirrel familiar, Tansy, came scurrying into the office. Lucky thing got to play out in the garden all day while I was stuck indoors, but she never failed to come and rescue me as soon as the day was over.

I studied the clock on Chloe's desk in feigned surprise,

as if I hadn't been watching it out of the corner of my eye for the better part of the day. "Would you look at that. It's time to go home."

Grandma tutted. "We'll pick this up again tomorrow."

"No, we won't. It's the weekend."

"You're Head Witch. You—"

"Don't get weekends off. I get it." I smiled sweetly at her. "However, the rest of the coven members certainly do, so there are no meetings on my schedule. Chloe has already handled the necessary paperwork for the week, haven't you?"

Chloe herself looked up from her desk, having kept working without acknowledging the time. "I have, yes."

My assistant was the definition of the word "efficient," and I frankly had no idea how she had managed to keep her focus on paperwork while Grandma attempted to instruct me in magic. Even when I'd levitated the entire office into the air, she'd kept typing away at her laptop, and I had the suspicion that she might have been sitting on the rim of an active volcano and would continue to fill out paperwork.

I, however, got antsy if I spent more than ten minutes in a chair at a time. There was a reason I'd picked being a magical courier as my low-paying job of choice, and it said volumes for how excruciating Grandma's magic lessons were that I'd have rather spent an extra hour at my desk instead.

Grandma gave a long-suffering sigh. "Nobody respects me anymore."

Her ghost vanished in the same instant as my phone buzzed. Tansy hopped onto the desk, while I scooped up my phone to find a message from Harvey Walton. "I'm invited to a party. Tonight."

"Ooh," said Tansy. "What's the occasion?"

"The oldest member of the Sky Hopper team is retiring." I skimmed the message's contents. "I guess Harvey and the others are going to see him off in style. Excellent excuse for a party, in my opinion."

Tansy tilted her head to one side. "You think your mother will happily let you go?"

"I have the evening off. And the weekend. Not that I'm planning to get absolutely trashed, but there's no reason whatsoever for her to object."

"I beg to differ," Carmilla said from across the room. "You should be preparing for the week ahead of you."

"*You* plan to sleep all weekend," I pointed out. "Besides, getting to know how Wildwood Heath has changed in the past few years is a part of my job as well."

Carmilla sprang off the desk and coughed up a giant hairball on the carpet. I was willing to bet she'd done that just so I'd have to clean it up instead of leaving the office, but it backfired. Closing her laptop, Chloe rose to her feet and gave me a sympathetic look. "I'll clean that up. You head home to get ready for the party—you've earned it."

Ignoring Carmilla's noise of derision—or possibly the appearance of another hairball—I waved to my assistant and followed Tansy to the door. "Thanks, Chloe. Please don't do any paperwork over the weekend. In fact, if I see you near the office before Monday morning, I'll send Tansy to crap in your shoes."

Chloe's shy smile became a grin. "I'll keep that in mind."

Sorted. My mother had made a great choice in

assigning her as my assistant, but I sometimes worried that Chloe worked as hard as she did partly out of fear of retaliation from certain family members of mine. Which was not my style. I might have to deal with the derision as a result, but I'd rather be mocked than get a reputation as an ogre who rained terror down upon her subordinates.

"I am *not* going to crap in her shoes," Tansy said as we left the office. "I'm far more house-trained than that."

"I had to persuade her somehow," I replied. "Did I mention I caught her doing paperwork in the hallway when my office door was locked the other day?"

"She's enthusiastic. That's a good thing. It'll keep your grandmother off your back, right?"

"Not quite. I still have to learn to use this." I twirled the sceptre between my hands in demonstration and narrowly avoided dropping it on Tansy. "Oops. Sorry."

She ran ahead of me with a squeaking noise. "Be glad she didn't see you do that. You're sure your mother won't raise a fuss about this party?"

"I'll deploy the same argument. It's for the good of the coven that I socialise with my fellow townspeople."

It wasn't exactly the Head Witch's responsibility to fraternise with the local sports teams, of course, but the party was outside of office hours. In fact, since the Head Witch was the highest authority among the covens, I could theoretically change the timetable so that I got to sleep all day and work all night if I were so inclined, but I stuck to the coven's preferred schedule to make things easier for everyone else. Let nobody say I was unwilling to compromise, despite my own plans being majorly uprooted by my sudden and accidental attainment of the title of Head Witch.

Less than a month ago, my overriding goal had been to earn enough from my courier job to buy a proper camera. Instead, I'd been gifted said camera as a bribe to move back into my childhood home and play at being Head Witch for the next six months to a year, depending on how long it took to fulfil whatever task the sceptre had chosen me for. Putting the future of the region's covens in the hands of an inanimate object whose motives nobody fully understood didn't strike me as particularly sensible, but the sceptre generally chose a wielder who was experienced in running a coven. Not the family screwup.

Whatever its reasons, once I was done with whatever task I had to handle, I was more than happy to hand the sceptre over to my mother, aka, the leader of the Wildwood Coven and the person who actually deserved the position, though she'd accepted my unexpected new status with far more grace and dignity than her sister had. But that wouldn't spare me the inevitable lecture when she found out I was heading to a party with the leader of the local Sky Hopper team, so I speed-walked home to avoid her catching up to me on her way out of the office.

Upon reaching the large manor house that my mother had inherited a few weeks ago, I unlocked the door and let Tansy scamper ahead of me into the carpeted hall. While I hadn't intended to end up living in my childhood home again at twenty-five, this was a temporary measure, necessitated by my new title. It wasn't worth finding a new place to move into for only a few months before I left the town once again, after all.

Tansy scurried into the kitchen, her bright tail sticking up in the air. "When's the party?"

I checked the time. "I'll leave in an hour."

"Good. I have some pigeons to chase." She sprinted towards the door to the back garden, where she enjoyed running up and down the bird feeders and chasing the local wildlife, much to the annoyance of Horace, Mum's long-suffering familiar.

Meanwhile, I retreated to my room to decide what to wear. Unlike when I attended coven-related societal functions, I wouldn't be required to dress up, but it wouldn't do for the Head Witch to go out wearing skimpy clubbing attire. I'd be hard-pressed to avoid an argument with my mother over this as it was, so I settled on a short denim skirt and a purple top that wasn't too low cut and then applied a little makeup. Mascara and eyeshadow, a little lipstick, nothing too over the top. Mum and Ramsey would think otherwise, of course, but considering the fuss my cartoonish socks caused whenever I wore them to the office, it'd be a no-win scenario if I decided to go in a hoodie and jeans instead.

With my outfit in place, I picked up my new camera and tucked it into my shoulder bag, figuring I might as well take it for a spin. After I'd put on my heeled shoes, I left the sceptre in its case beside my bed and made my way quietly downstairs.

Typically, as I reached the hallway, Mum waylaid me from the living room. Instead of asking, "Where are you going?" she began with, "Why are you leaving the sceptre behind?"

"Because I've been invited to a party at the Fox's Den, and I want it to be safe while I'm gone," I replied.

"You think it'd be safer here than with you?"

"I won't need it. If I need to use magic, I can just use my wand."

Her eyes narrowed. "The Head Witch is always a target."

"I'm aware of that." Okay, there was the—admittedly slim—chance someone might try to bump me off while my guard was down, but the sceptre wouldn't necessarily be a deterrent, and if I carried it with me, I'd lose any hope of anonymity. "I'm meeting people there, Mum. I won't be alone."

She tutted. "And who might those *people* be?"

"Harvey, from the local Sky Hopper team."

Her nostrils flared. "The one you went to school with, right? You were with him at the party after the familiar contest, weren't you?"

There was no reason for the accusatory tone, considering said party had only been possible because I'd caught and helped jail my would-be murderer that very evening. "Harvey is the team's captain. And he coaches at the academy. I think you'd like him."

"I'm sure he's perfectly nice," she said in tones that implied the very opposite. "However, he's not a suitable romantic partner for a Head Witch."

She'd never even *met* him, but her mind had been made up the moment he'd failed to show sufficient status befitting someone of my supposed stature. Never mind that she herself had married someone from a lesser coven, pulling him out of obscurity and into an unpleasant spotlight in the process. While I had zero desire for Harvey to suffer the same indignities as my dad had while he'd been married to my mother, she was way ahead of herself if she thought I was contemplating anything serious like *marrying* the guy. For one thing, I wasn't even supposed to be staying in Wildwood Heath for the long term. Harvey knew that too.

"I didn't say anything about him being a romantic partner," I said pointedly. "But since I won't be Head Witch forever, I'm sure you can tolerate him for the time being."

"You shouldn't speak like that," she reprimanded. "Many people would kill to be in your position."

"I'm aware, since I've already been on the receiving end of several murder attempts." If anything, my brushes with death had only nudged me towards being more determined to live while I had the chance. "Besides, I didn't think *you* wanted me to keep the title."

"That's not for me to decide, Robin."

I suppressed an eye roll. "Yes, I know the sceptre makes its own decisions, but that doesn't mean I need to get attached to it. Would you rather I spent all my free time hiding in my room, huddling over the sceptre like Gollum with the One Ring?"

Tansy scurried down the hall to join me. "You wouldn't. You don't have the patience to stay indoors for that long."

Nice to know my familiar had faith in me... though she had a point.

"There are two extremes." Mum eyed the feathers Tansy scattered in her wake with disapproval. "I'm not asking you to be like the Head Witches who refused to give up their magic either."

I blinked, surprised. "I didn't know anyone did."

Granted, she'd probably told me at some point, but my memories of my childhood lessons were patchy at best, and I'd hardly thought I'd ever find myself in my indomitable grandmother's shoes.

"It's not unheard of." Mum pursed her lips. "Suffice to say that I'm glad none of the people in our town who possess those tendencies ended up carrying the sceptre."

"Like Aunt Shannon or Vanessa." My aunt and cousin were scheming enough that they'd willingly turned against their own family members in order to procure the sceptre, and Aunt Shannon had been livid when I'd claimed it instead. "They didn't though, and you don't need to worry about anything like that from me."

There was no chance I'd get too attached to the sceptre to ever give it up, but for many, it wasn't the sceptre itself that they wanted but power in both the magical and political senses. Even Grandma had been tenacious enough to try to cling to the sceptre even in death.

As for me? I fit in with my family like a square peg in a round hole, and it had stunned everyone that I'd been selected due to possessing something they didn't—even though I wasn't entirely certain what that was yet.

Mum waved her wand, and the feathers Tansy had dropped vanished from sight. "We're all adjusting, including you. I wish you'd rethink tonight. You're still in a vulnerable position."

I put on a reassuring tone. "I won't be alone, and the staff at the Fox's Den won't stand for any trouble. I go there all the time, remember? I just want one night where I can just… not think about people staring at me all the time."

"You're never free from attention, Robin."

"Yes, but that isn't anything new." Even as a child, I'd been a target of stares and whispers based on my status as the former Head Witch's granddaughter. It might be an illusion, but the absence of the sceptre in my hand would make me feel less like a boulder lay on my neck and shoulders for a brief while.

"It's different now," Mum insisted. "People will take notice of every event you attend, every person you choose to spend time with, and judge the entire coven as a result. The entire *town*, in fact."

"Like I said—same old."

Mum, who wouldn't know a social life if it sprouted in her prized flower bed, had always been blissfully unaware of how it felt to walk around with the magical world's equivalent of the paparazzi on one's tail. She hadn't ventured outside Wildwood Heath in years herself.

Mum sighed. "Really, Robin."

"Look, it's not like I'm going to a strip club or an orgy, or…" I broke off before Mum could look even more scandalised than she already did. "It's a pub. That's all. I won't be out all night, and I won't embarrass you. Also, if I don't have the sceptre, I'll be less likely to use its magic and accidentally turn someone into a statue again."

"That's still happening?"

"On occasion. Like I said—I have my wand."

"Fine," she said. "Let me know if anything happens. *Anything.* Clear?"

"Right."

Not likely. I didn't think she'd want to know the details if, say, Harvey and I ended up making out. Which, if I admitted it, was precisely how I hoped the night would end. My entire family, save for my dad, was completely allergic to the very concept of the word "fun."

When it came to Harvey… Mum might not think him

a likely romantic prospect, but it was because he didn't care that I was Head Witch that I'd continued to be drawn to him even after the recent upheavals in my life. Mum's own marriage to Dad had gone against tradition, though my dad had dealt with no end of ridicule from the other witches and the press both during their marriage and after their eventual separation. He seemed much happier with his new partner, Jessica, who had two kids of her own. Whether that was a sore point with Mum I didn't know, but it was Ramsey who'd held the longest grudge against him for leaving.

Families were messy, even the ones which didn't involve powerful covens and long-standing magical feuds, but I couldn't help wondering what my life would have been like if I could have just gone out for a night of flirting with a cute guy without the spectre of my new title hanging over my head.

At least I'd won the argument. When the door closed behind me, Tansy broke into a skip straight away, but I managed to refrain from joining in—at least until I was sure Mum wasn't watching me from the window.

2

With my new camera in hand and a smile on my face, I entered the Fox's Den. The cosy pub was one of the few places in Wildwood Heath where all kinds of paranormals mingled in harmony without the usual rivalries and tensions, unless you counted occasional arguments over sports, magical and otherwise. Werewolves and other shifters were the most common patrons, but there were plenty of witches and wizards, too, as well as the odd vampire, fairy, and goblin.

Today though, most of the pub was devoted to the Sky Hopper team and its fans. A sea of bright red greeted me, with the team still dressed in their vibrant uniforms and their supporters of all ages draped in crimson scarves despite the relatively warm weather. I ducked underneath a bright banner embossed with the team's weird bird-shaped mascot and made my way to the table, where the team was boisterously celebrating with mugs of beer. Upon seeing me, Harvey jovially elbowed his way to my side. Tall and broad, he had red confetti in his windswept dark hair and wore his crimson uniform, his captain's badge decorated with the same bird emblem that adorned every banner and badge in the pub.

"You came." He grinned at me, a beer already in his hand. "Glad you could make it."

"Same here." I gestured to his badge. "I never asked—what kind of bird is that?"

He glanced down briefly. "A dodo."

"Why do you have an extinct bird as your team's emblem?"

"That's a question for our retiring captain." He beckoned me towards the table, where the rest of the team sat expectantly. "Come and introduce yourself to everyone, Robin."

"Doesn't everyone already know who I am?" I wasn't carrying the sceptre, admittedly, and half the team had been drinking heavily already. "All right, but I'm not doing any party tricks."

"No danger of that. Jansen here is the star attraction." He grabbed a spare chair and moved it beside his own, indicating for me to sit down. I did so, bracing myself for stares, but everyone seemed far more interested in singing team songs and tossing red confetti at one another.

"Hey, there." A burly player with dark skin and a mischievous smile spotted me. "Are you Harvey's friend, Robin? The one he's always talking about?"

"He talks about me?" Heat crept up my neck as if I were a schoolgirl with a crush, though it was more to do with the mental image of the expressions on my family members' faces if they knew the entire Sky Hopper team was aware that Harvey and I were potential romantic interests than anything else.

"All the time." He nudged Harvey in the arm. "I'm Cole. Hey, everyone, this is Robin."

All eyes turned on me, and I forced a smile. "Nice to meet you all."

"You've met our captain already, of course, but that's his predecessor, Jansen." Cole pointed at a man with grey streaks in his tangled dark hair and a nose that looked like it'd been broken several times, either from falling off a broomstick or being hit by a rampaging Sky Hopper player. "He stepped down as captain a year ago but stayed on the team as one of the Falcons. Right, Jansen?"

At being addressed directly, Jansen looked blearily at me and spoke in a gravelly voice. "Nice to meet you."

Harvey continued with the introductions, pointing towards a heavyset girl with a few recent-looking bruises on her pale face and a smaller girl next to her with braided hair and a notably chipped front tooth. "This is Gwen and Everly—they're Vultures."

I nodded in understanding. To win a game of Sky Hopper, a team needed to pass a certain number of hoops along a row of broomstick-riding players referred to as the Falcons—without falling prey to the Vultures, whose role was to swipe the other team's hoops and take them for their own. Straightforward enough to remember, even for someone who didn't religiously follow the game.

"Tomas is over at the bar." Everly pointed across the pub. "He's sulking because he got knocked out during our last match. We won, but his ego took a beating."

"Poor thing," Gwen said without much sympathy in her tone. "He's the reason I got these bruises from the other team's leading Falcon. He should have had my back when I swiped the hoop, but instead, the guy clobbered me while Tomas was looking the other way."

Ouch. Fighting dirty wasn't strictly allowed, but that didn't mean people didn't break the rules when the game got heated. Same as any sport, really. Harvey didn't look to have suffered any injuries, but the captain was typically positioned at the very back of the row of players, since he had to survive long enough to claim the last of the hoops and declare victory. That also meant he was more likely to get injured at the end of the game rather than the start, compared to the other Falcons. No wonder Jansen looked slightly cross-eyed, considering he'd captained the team for a decade or more.

Cole continued introducing the various team members, while I did my best to take it all in. I'd grown used to memorising people's names and faces after the last couple of weeks as Head Witch, though so far, the players seemed to be far less judgemental than certain covens were known to be.

Harvey finished the introductions by pointing to a member who was so short his head barely showed above the table. "And this is Gabriel, who'll be taking Jansen's place on the team."

Gabriel looked up from his position next to Jansen and mumbled, "Hey."

At the bar, the player they'd called Tomas shot a dirty look in the newcomer's direction for some reason. Gabriel shrank back in his seat, and a flash of fluffy red tail caught my eye from where Tansy was in the process of stealing a cherry from someone's cocktail glass. I beckoned to her with a pointed stare, and she scampered to my side, not looking contrite in the slightest.

"Oh, you have a squirrel familiar?" Everly's gaze followed her across the table. "A *red* squirrel?"

"She most definitely does," answered Tansy. Since nobody here but me could understand her, they'd have just heard a squeaking noise but one loud enough to draw the attention of the entire table.

"Oh, I love squirrels," Everly gushed. "Look at her."

"She's adorable," put in Gwen.

Everyone cooed over Tansy for a good five minutes while she scampered over the table and displayed her fluffy red tail for everyone to see, enjoying the attention. When someone brought the next round of drinks over, she returned to my shoulder. "I could get used to this."

I gave her an eye roll. "Don't let it go to your head."

In truth, I was relieved she'd been the centre of attention instead of me, as it made it easier to maintain the illusion that I wasn't Head Witch for the duration of the evening. It didn't hurt that everyone was more fixated on the Sky Hopper team than on me being in their company, and whenever someone recognised my face, Tansy was more than happy to distract them. The evening passed swiftly, and once we'd finished our meals, someone brought out a sponge cake decorated with the team's emblem.

"Why *did* you pick a dodo?" I asked Harvey. "What did Jansen say, something about a bet?"

"The team was buried in the ground before I became captain," Jansen said, overhearing. His voice was considerably slurred by this point. "We brought it back from extinction."

"Er… I think the dodo is still extinct." I kept my voice quiet enough that only Harvey could hear me, not wanting to kill the mood. Not that anything would quell the team's spirit, despite the imminent departure of the former captain. "Unless I've missed some major news."

"It is." Harvey leaned over to speak to me in a low voice. "However, the phoenix was already taken by another team, so Jansen took the next-best available choice. I think it's quite distinctive as far as emblems go."

"He's not wrong," Tansy whispered in my ear. "Also, have you forgotten your camera? Might be the time for a team photo."

"Good call." Pulling out my new camera, I offered to take a group photo of the team members, and Cole and Harvey repeated the call until everyone was in the frame. Kind of. As far as photographs went, it wasn't my best, what with half the team too drunk to stand by this point. Still, I captured the mood pretty well, and Cole took the opportunity to call everyone to attention.

"Come on, let's start on the cake." He raised his voice over the general chatter. "It's Jansen's party, so he can cut the first slice. Ready?"

Someone handed Jansen a knife. His grip was a little unsteady, but nobody seemed bothered that he was hacking the cake into uneven pieces. As the others passed around plates and began distributing the slices, Jansen made a sudden choking noise and dropped his slice of cake. His face had gone purple, and everyone descended on him in alarm, questions clashing in the air.

Jansen writhed in his seat, hands flailing, until his coughing halted abruptly.

"He's dead!" Everly screamed.

Everyone stared at the former captain for an instant, horror-struck. Then chaos broke out, shouts echoing through the pub, panic spreading like a quick-acting fire.

"The cake's poisoned!" someone wailed. "He's dead!"

"Nobody else ate any of it, did they?" That was Harvey, looking wildly around the pub at the other team members. "Did they?"

Several murmurs of "no" followed, though several people had already thrown down their plates, and others had leapt clean out of their seats and away from what was left of the dodo-shaped cake. Questions shot back and forth like Sky Hopper hoops, while the poor werewolf working behind the bar clearly didn't know how to handle the ruckus. When his shouts for calm went unheard, he grabbed his phone, no doubt to call the police.

That ought to have been a sign for me to leave, considering I knew exactly who'd be leading the police's team, but I didn't want to leave Harvey's side. I stood firmly at his shoulder as he called out orders and attempted to wrangle the team back into order.

"They won't listen." He swore under his breath, his distraught gaze landing on Jansen's slumped position in his seat. "We have to get him out of here."

Cole joined him, equally shaken. "I didn't know. I wouldn't have asked him to cut the first slice if I'd known—"

"It's not your fault," Harvey reassured him. "None of us knew."

Then who killed him? The question ricocheted through my mind without connecting with an answer—until, inevitably, the door flew open, heralding the police's arrival at the pub. My brother, Ramsey, strode to the front of their group, his hedgehog familiar, Prickles, perched on his shoulder, and both of them stared judgementally at everyone. Or specifically, me, because my brother had picked me out of the crowd in an instant.

A clamour of voices rose from among players and supporters alike, and Ramsey held up a hand for silence. "Everyone sit down."

"There aren't enough chairs!" slurred a particularly drunk patron, who'd slumped against the side of the bar.

This did, unfortunately, seem to be the case. The crowd had doubled over the course of the evening, and it didn't help that the floor was covered in spilled beer and trampled bits of cake. While the rest of the police attempted to corral the various groups of drunken fans into some kind of order, Ramsey's gaze snagged on me at once. "Robin. Come with me."

Whispers rose from around me as the crowd began to put two and two together—some of them only now realising my identity.

Harvey gave my hand a reassuring squeeze. "Go with your brother."

"I'll see you later," I murmured, not wanting to say more in front of the crowd.

Thanks for that one, Ramsey.

I knew an escape route when I saw it though, so I forced my way to the door, wincing whenever someone elbowed me in the side or trod on my feet. When the cold night air hit my face, Ramsey seized my arm and tried to pull me the rest of the way out.

I snatched my arm out of his grip and hissed through clenched teeth. "You do realise that anyone who saw us will think you're either playing favourites or that I'm the prime suspect?"

He dropped his hand. "You're Head Witch. You should never have been there to begin with, not if you want to avoid a scandal."

"You're kidding, right?" Nope, he was deadly serious. "The only scandal here is that a man died, not that the Head Witch went to the pub on a Friday night."

"We have a reputation to uphold. *You* have a reputation."

"Yes, imagine what a tragedy it would be if the press found out." Honestly. "I can't imagine the Wildwood Coven would ever survive the shame."

"Go home," he told me.

"Do your job then," I retaliated. "Because you, unlike me, are supposed to be working at the moment, not worrying about my *reputation*."

Before I said anything more that I'd regret, I beckoned Tansy to follow me down the dark high street. My breath came quickly, hands curling into fists at my sides, and it didn't escape my attention that the hooting of owls and the barking of foxes followed me home as the wildlife responded to the wave of rage-fuelled magic leaking out of me.

"This is why I didn't want to carry the sceptre." I ducked a low-flying bat before it hit me in the face. "My magic has enough potential for disaster without being amplified."

Tansy waited for me to catch her up. "How do you always end up in these situations?"

"You mean running into murderers?" I folded my arms, shivering a little without the warmth of the pub cocooning me. "I wasn't even the target this time. It was pure bad luck."

"You're sure of that?"

"Yes," I answered firmly. "The cake was probably prepared ages before the party, let alone before Harvey asked me to go with him, and it's the first time I've been invited to any Sky Hopper-related event at all. The person responsible couldn't have known I'd be there when they concocted his murder."

Why murder someone who'd already retired from the team, anyway? I didn't know the Sky Hopper players well, but if any of them had had objections to Jansen as a player, murdering him at his retirement party was a hell of a weird time to act on their old grudges. That broom had already taken flight.

I forced the question of the murderer's identity to the back of my mind with difficulty. Ramsey would handle the investigation, and after our clash earlier, I doubted he'd welcome my input on the matter. He might have had an understandable reaction to me showing up at a crime scene *again,* but being able to understand the reasons for his behaviour didn't make me any less irritated that he'd painted a target on my head in front of the entire Sky Hopper team as well as everyone else in the pub. If anyone had somehow been unaware of my Head Witch status, it was a safe bet that the brief moment of anonymity had been thoroughly buried.

I speed-walked until my temper cooled then unlocked the front door to the house. Typically, Mum occupied the living room, reading through paperwork on the sofa with Horace and Carmilla napping on either side of her.

"Have a good night?" she asked without looking up.

I debated giving a noncommittal answer and then going to bed and leaving Ramsey to explain when he eventually got back, but he'd be out all night at this rate, and I'd only provoke her ire if I opted against telling her right away.

"It started well." I halted in the doorway to the living room. "Then someone poisoned one of the team's Falcons with his own farewell cake."

Mum still didn't look up from her paperwork. "What exactly is a Falcon?"

"Did you miss the part where I said he was poisoned?" I asked. "The Falcon is a position on the Sky Hopper team. The guy was retiring tonight, but someone decided to make his retirement permanent."

She briefly lifted her head, her brows drawing together. "I take it Ramsey is there?"

"For the foreseeable future." I suppressed an eye roll. "Poor Jansen. It was his party, and someone killed him."

"He let his guard down, I'd guess," Carmilla said sleepily from the sofa.

"You're all far too relaxed about this." They'd be singing a different song if it was *me* who'd been targeted by the killer, but I had an inkling that despite their cavalier attitudes, I'd have a harder time on my next attempt to leave the house without the sceptre.

Mum returned to her paperwork. "Ramsey will get to the bottom of it, I don't doubt."

I could translate that as "Don't get involved, Robin." Fair enough. It wasn't any of my business. Ramsey had made that clear enough already. I felt bad for Harvey, of course, especially as he was the captain of the team and the one who'd end up having to deal with the fallout, but that didn't mean my brother would be content to let me offer my own opinion.

"Speaking of Ramsey, can you let him know that he shouldn't treat me any differently to anyone else?"

This time, she looked at me properly. "What did you do?"

"Nothing whatsoever. He more or less dragged me out of the pub and sent me on my merry way like a drunk being chucked out at closing time. If he wanted to avoid drawing unnecessary attention to me, then he completely failed."

"He can't help worrying about you."

It seemed to me that "worrying" usually translated as "acting like a condescending twit" as far as Ramsey was concerned.

"I'm not the one who's lying dead in a plateful of cake."

I had a sense that winning one argument was enough for a single day, so I made for the stairs and headed up to my room.

"She has a point." Tansy scampered ahead of me to the glass case in which I'd stored the sceptre for safekeeping, next to a bookcase bursting with my childhood manga collection. "I'd take the sceptre with you next time."

"I'm pretty sure even the sceptre can't remove poison when someone's already swallowed it." Not without requiring medical knowledge that I lacked, anyway. "I'll give Ramsey the benefit of the doubt this once, but if he tries it again, you're welcome to crap in *his* shoes."

I unpacked my bag, a pang of guilt hitting me when I pulled out the camera Ramsey had given me. Partly a bribe, yes, but also a gift and a rare show of pride in my achievements.

Right. I'd apologise tomorrow morning. Not least because it might convince him to tell me the details of how the questioning had gone and if he'd managed to find the killer among the celebrating crowd. For Harvey's sake, I hoped so. This certainly wasn't how I'd hoped for the night to end.

3

Ramsey didn't return until the following morning, when he entered the kitchen while I was eating breakfast at the table. I'd spent half the night completely unable to sleep, so I'd had plenty of time to rehearse my apology, but he spoke first. "Please tell me Kimberly made coffee."

"You're in luck." I indicated the breakfast laid out on the table. "It isn't even cold yet."

Kimberly had left enough for everyone. While some might call it unnecessary to hire a chef for a family as small as ours, the fact that none of us could even make toast without causing a disaster was a good enough reason to outsource that particular task. Pity I had yet to convince them to view paperwork in the same way.

"Good." Ramsey poured himself a mug of coffee, leaning against the counter rather than sitting at the table with me. Maybe he hadn't entirely forgotten our argument the previous evening.

"Rough night?" I tried to inject sympathy into my tone.

His gaze slid towards me with more than a little suspicion, though he'd have been right if he'd guessed that I wanted to know how the investigation had gone. "You already know the answer to that, Robin."

"Just making conversation." I'd already forgotten my rehearsed apologies for my comments the previous evening, but they'd come out sounding less than sincere at this point anyway. My brother and I didn't do emotional talk. "I think Mum stayed up late waiting for you."

He drank half of his coffee in one swig. "She knows how long these cases take to solve. I'm heading back to the office later anyway."

"Without sleeping first?" I brushed crumbs off my lap. "Can't the rest of your team take over?"

He put down his coffee mug and tipped some milk into a saucer for Prickles. The little hedgehog perched on the table and lapped at the saucer's contents. Even his familiar had impeccable manners, at least compared to Tansy, who'd been attempting to wrestle a pigeon away from the bird feeder the last time I'd seen her. "There aren't enough of us. Besides, it's my job."

If I hadn't known better, I'd say that was a jab at me for my comment the previous day, though like Mum and Grandma, he refused to delegate if he could help it. "It's not your job to handle everything alone."

"I'm running the department single-handedly at the moment, since three people are away for the weekend, so technically, it *is* my job."

"Anything I can help with?"

His gaze flickered towards me again. "Not at the moment."

"No need to look at me like that." I picked up a third

piece of toast. "I have nothing else going on this weekend, that's all."

"You don't work for the police force, Robin."

"I was *at* the party," I pointed out. "Theoretically, I'm a witness, despite how quickly you removed me from the crime scene."

He pinched the bridge of his nose. "Maybe I acted hastily, but if you hadn't been there, I wouldn't have had to make that call."

So much for avoiding another argument. "If I hadn't been there, then you wouldn't have at least one witness you know for sure wasn't involved in the murder. You're welcome."

His face reddened a little. "You might have easily been the victim instead."

"If I'd taken the first slice of cake, you mean?" I suppressed a shudder. "I mean, you aren't wrong, but there were a ton of people in that pub. It's not a very efficient way to commit murder, poisoning a cake that everyone was going to eat."

"It wasn't poisoned."

"What?" I put down my uneaten slice of toast. "Then how did Jansen die?"

"He choked to death on a badge that someone put into his slice of cake. The badge was shaped like a bird."

"The team's mascot." My throat went dry. "Wait... a badge from someone's uniform?"

He grunted and said nothing, but he didn't need to. I'd seen the same badge up close at least a dozen times.

I studied my brother's tense posture. "You're not telling me something."

"What would give you that idea?"

"You're wearing that expression that makes you look like you sat on Prickles."

A muscle ticked in his jaw. "I'm not supposed to discuss this with you. Forget I said anything."

A sudden suspicion dawned on me. "Whose badge, exactly, did he choke to death on?"

Silence.

"Ramsey?"

His reluctant answer: "The captain's."

"Not... not Harvey's?" My jaw dropped. "You can't be serious."

"I knew you'd be upset if I said anything," he said, maddeningly calm. Well, he would be, because it wasn't his potential romantic partner who was in danger of getting accused of murder. "The badge was from his spare uniform, not the one he was wearing, but it was definitely the captain's."

"Then someone else might have brought it with them," I said. "Come on. Harvey wouldn't have ripped up his own uniform even if he'd committed murder. Which he didn't."

"I don't work based on conjecture but facts."

"Then have you questioned him yet?" I asked. "Or is that the plan for today?"

"I'm not supposed to share the details of the investigation."

"Don't blame me." I pushed back from the table. "You gave me the information voluntarily, remember?"

He rubbed his eyes with the back of his hand. "Clearly, I shouldn't have."

I should have seen that one coming, but he couldn't possibly believe Harvey was the killer. No way. "I'm not trying to muscle in on your investigation. I wouldn't be asking questions at all if you weren't accusing an innocent man."

"I'm not accusing anyone." He drank the rest of his coffee, picked up a piece of toast, and beckoned to his familiar to follow him. "Please try to stay out of trouble."

Prickles hopped off the table, and the two left the kitchen.

"Good morning to you too," I said to his retreating back.

I'd never intended to get involved in the investigation, but I had zero intention of letting Harvey be the one who took the blame for the murder. Thoroughly irked, I went looking for Tansy out in the back garden.

Upon spotting me across the flower beds, Tansy scurried over from the bird feeder to join me. "Did you and Ramsey make it up?"

"No," I said sourly. "He thinks *Harvey* is the murderer."

"He thinks *what?*"

I glared into Mum's prized flower beds. "He decided that since Harvey is the owner of the badge that Jansen choked to death on, he's the murderer."

"What badge? I thought he was poisoned."

"Apparently not." I turned back towards the house. "I doubt pestering Ramsey will change his mind, but he thinks the facts speak for themselves."

Tansy tilted her head. "Which means you're going to talk to Piper and discuss how to prove otherwise."

She knew me too well. "I'll see if she's awake first."

I fired off a message to Piper. Mum gave her the weekends off from tending the gardens, so I'd wondered if she might be asleep, but she replied to my message right away and agreed to meet with me at the local café. Sorted.

I went to grab my shoes and then left the house. Since I hadn't seen Mum yet, she must be at the office to do yet more unnecessary work for the coven that nobody would be in the slightest bit grateful for. Though at least I'd avoided another lecture on my favoured haunts, since like the Fox's Den, my mother didn't consider Were's My Coffee? a suitable place for the Head Witch to spend her free time.

With Tansy at my side, I left the enclave where the biggest witch families in town made their homes and made my way to the high street. The winding road contained an eclectic array of small shops and cafés; like most magical rural communities, Wildwood Heath prided itself on supporting local businesses. The werewolf-run café fit right in among its neighbours, and I breathed in the pleasant smell of coffee as I pushed open the door. A magpie took flight at my back, and I halted momentarily in case it turned out to be Myrtle, Aunt Shannon's familiar. When the bird didn't return, I continued into the café.

Rowan was on her shift that morning, and she waved at me from behind the counter, humming under her breath. My cousin seemed much happier working at the café than she'd been when she'd had to live at home with her mother, my ever-scheming Aunt Shannon.

"What can I get you?" she asked in her bubbly barista voice.

"A latte, please. I like the hair."

My cousin had finally taken the long-awaited step of dyeing her bottle-blond hair a vivid shade of pink, bright enough that it hurt to look at—though it still wasn't as bright as her mother's face would turn if she set eyes on her youngest daughter.

Rowan grinned. "You were just thinking of what my mum would look like if she saw it, right?"

"Guilty. In fairness, I know people who would pay to witness the ugly fallout."

Or pay *not* to witness it. Aunt Shannon had made no secret of the fact that she favoured Vanessa, her eldest child, and that Rowan was the spare. Hardly a nice way to treat your kid, but the fact that she'd cut off Rowan's allowance and effectively trapped her at home had crossed a line. It'd been the money Rowan had inherited from our grandmother that had enabled her to move to a flat above the café and start over, and I was thrilled to see how well it was going so far.

"Were some of those people at the party, by any chance?" Rowan remarked. "Once I get off my shift, I wanna hear all about it."

"How did you know I was there?"

She rolled her eyes, handing me my latte. "Because the Sky Hopper team was at your favourite pub. I'd be surprised if you *weren't* there."

"Despite my mother's best efforts."

Rowan pulled a face. "What did she do, try to guilt-trip you? She ought to know you're capable of making your own choices."

"Supposedly, the Head Witch makes choices that reflect on the entire coven, the entire town, and possibly the entire country as well. Going to the pub is not a respectable activity, according to her."

She snorted. "I don't miss the constant judgement, I can tell you that much."

"I bet." I cast a brief glance towards the door, recalling the bird I'd seen outside. "You haven't seen your mother at all? Or her familiar?"

"My mother made it clear I'm not welcome in her home. I've seen magpies outside the café a few times, but they're common enough."

"Still." Aunt Shannon's familiar, Myrtle, was notorious for eavesdropping on people, especially her own family members, but spying on Rowan in her new life was underhanded to say the least. If I asked my aunt outright if she'd sent her familiar to watch her youngest daughter from afar, she'd deny doing anything of the sort, so I put it out of my mind for now.

The door jangled open, and Piper entered the café. My best friend was casually dressed for her day off in jeans and a hoodie, and she gave Rowan a nod of acknowledgement. The two of them had clashed a few weeks ago over an interview with the press in which Rowan had shared our family's secrets and unintentionally made me into a target in the process. I'd had an easier time forgiving Rowan than my best friend had, but she was trying.

"I'll have one of those." Piper gestured at my latte, speaking in neutral if not friendly tones.

"Coming right up." Rowan went to make Piper's drink, while I picked out a table next to the counter and then launched straight into explaining the events of the previous evening.

"I wondered why the party ended early," Piper remarked. "I got an early night, since I had a migraine, so I couldn't make it to the pub. I'm not close friends with anyone on the team anyway, but it looked fun."

"It was, until the guy who the party was supposed to be celebrating choked to death on a badge, of all things."

"A badge?" Rowan returned with Piper's drink. "I thought he was poisoned."

"Who told you that?"

"I've overheard three conversations this morning alone between people who heard what happened," Rowan said. "I guess the police couldn't haul every single attendee to the station for questioning, so they sent them home."

No wonder Ramsey had seen it as a necessity to return to work as soon as possible. "Sounds like it's going to take a while to sort this one out. My brother came home for about ten minutes and said that Jansen choked on a badge, not poison."

"I'm surprised he told you anything at all," Rowan commented.

"Same." Piper swiped her drink and set it down on the table. "He must have been in a good mood."

"Nah, he was sleep deprived and stressed out." I stirred my latte absently. "He said the badge belonged to *Harvey*. From his spare uniform, but he wouldn't entertain the idea that someone else stole it to kill the former captain."

Piper choked on her latte. "He can't be serious. He thinks *Harvey* is the killer?"

"Isn't Harvey the one who invited you to the party?" Rowan's eyes rounded.

"You've got it." I grimaced. "There's absolutely zero chance he's the killer, but Ramsey won't let my word count as evidence in his favour."

"Well, that's unfair," Piper said.

"Yeah," Rowan agreed. "I know he's the head of the

police force, but he must know that accusing your boyfriend—"

"He's not my boyfriend."

"Yet," Piper added. "Your brother will find the real culprit, I'm sure. It's his area of expertise."

"Sky Hopper definitely isn't." I returned my attention to my coffee. "Though I can't understand why someone would murder a retiring player."

"Personal grudge?" Piper suggested. "A whim? Drunken mishap?"

"Whoever it was, they stole Harvey's captain's badge." I looked up sharply as the door swung inward.

The freckled youth who entered the café was none other than Jansen's replacement on the Sky Hopper team. *Hmm.* I watched him approach the counter, his gaze darting around as if he expected my brother to appear behind him and arrest him.

"Why're you looking at that kid?" whispered Piper.

"He's the guy who the Sky Hopper team hired to replace the man who died yesterday." What was his name again? Gabriel? "I guess my brother isn't questioning him at the moment."

Rowan hastened to get back behind the counter and greeted the newcomer. "Hey, there. Want to order a drink?"

Gabriel saw me and paled, clearly recognising me from the party the day before. "I'll have a latte to go, please."

"What did you do to him?" Piper whispered in my ear.

"Nothing," I murmured back. "We barely exchanged three words, but I'm guessing Ramsey scared him yesterday."

"You should talk to him."

That would not be wise, but the kid was scared out of his mind, and I had the distinct impression that my brother was the reason for his terror. Come to think of it, I'd seen at least one team member look unimpressed at the new recruit chosen to take Jansen's place, and while I hadn't thought anything of it at the time, any tensions between the players might lead to the culprit.

I rose to my feet and approached the counter next to the newcomer. "Hey, Gabriel."

He jumped. "Hi, erm, Head Witch."

Hang on, was it *me* he was frightened of?

"I'm not here as Head Witch," I reassured him. "I mean, I'm just getting coffee with friends. Also, if my brother gave you a hard time yesterday, I can give him a stern talking-to."

He shook his head violently. "I don't want to get into trouble."

Bit late for that. "You won't. Ramsey is all talk, mostly, and he won't arrest anyone who hasn't committed a crime."

"I didn't," he mumbled to the counter. "I didn't kill Jansen."

"I believe you." Had someone accused him? Or was Ramsey being equally intimidating towards all the potential suspects? I debated asking how high on the suspect list he thought Harvey was, but equally strong was my desire to know the identity of the real culprit. "You have no reason to have killed a man who was already retiring, right?"

His shoulders relaxed a little. "Exactly. It happened so suddenly that I didn't realise what was going on at first."

"Same," I encouraged. "Poor Jansen. Did you have much chance to talk to him before he retired?"

"At the party? Not much."

"Was it him who picked you for the team?" I pressed. "Or was it a joint agreement?"

Rowan gave him his drink, which he picked up so shakily that some of the coffee slopped over the sides. "Jansen made the final call. I was surprised. I didn't think anyone would…"

As he trailed off, Piper leaned over and prodded me in the spine, while Tansy scampered up my shoulder and tickled my neck with her tail. I spun around to face the door—or, to be more precise, the man standing in the doorway, looking at me in disapproval.

Ramsey.

4

Ramsey glowered at me, one hand resting on the open door.

I gave him a wave, resigning myself to a repeat of yesterday's argument. "Hey, Ramsey."

"What are you doing?" he said between clenched teeth.

"Getting coffee with Piper." I gestured at the table. "And talking to Rowan."

"You mean talking to one of my suspects. I told you not to get involved."

"He's allowed to buy a coffee, Ramsey," I pointed out. "I didn't know he was going to walk in here." I glanced over my shoulder at Gabriel, who shrank back as if hoping the floor would swallow him up.

Ramsey followed my gaze. "You were questioning him yourself. Don't deny it."

"I'm not denying anything. If you were in my place, you'd have taken the opportunity to ask him a couple of questions too."

"I most certainly would not."

"Yes, you would," Tansy interjected. "Also, if you thought he was genuinely guilty, he'd already be in custody."

Ramsey scowled. "Nobody is in custody yet, at least not until we've finished taking statements from witnesses. But if you're seen talking to *any* of the suspects in public, it reflects badly on both of us."

"Half the town was at the party," I pointed out. "Also, did you say statements from witnesses?"

He hesitated for a second too long. "Yes, I did."

"I'm a witness." I tilted my head. "You know you never actually asked me what I saw at the party, don't you?"

He gave me a long-suffering look. "You just want to get in on my investigation."

"I want this solved," I corrected. "As much as you do, if not more."

For Harvey's sake, at least. If Ramsey kicked up a fuss about me talking to *him* in public, then we could say farewell to our temporary truce.

"If I let you come into the office, will you please refrain from getting under anyone's feet?" he asked.

"Only if *you* refrain from treating me any differently than you'd treat anyone else giving a statement on witnessing a crime," I responded. "Deal?"

Ramsey's gaze raked over me. "Deal."

"I'll be with you in five."

I returned to the table first to finish what was left of my latte, while Piper rolled her eyes at me. "Did you just talk your brother into letting you in on the investigation?"

"I'm a witness," I reminded her. "Besides, he's clearly in over his head."

Not that he'd ever admit it. The guy could be up to his

neck in a barrel full of alligators and would still insist he was in total control of the situation.

"So it has nothing whatsoever to do with getting Harvey off the hook so you can go on a proper date?" Rowan ventured.

"Chance would be a fine thing." I put down my empty coffee mug. "I can't even go to a party without someone dropping dead."

Piper snorted. "So you're going straight to the police station?"

"I shouldn't be more than an hour. I'll message you."

Gabriel, I noticed belatedly, had given us the slip. He must have darted out the door while I'd been occupied talking to Ramsey. Smart move if you asked me.

In the meantime, Tansy and I left the coffee shop and headed towards the police station. Tansy got there first and amused herself by setting off the automatic doors a few times before

Ramsey appeared and gave her a stern look. "Calm your familiar down, Robin."

"I'll behave." Tansy scurried up my leg and perched on my shoulder. "Where do you want us to wait?"

He pointed at a glass-topped door at the end of the reception area. "In the waiting room over there. Remember what I told you, Robin."

"Which part?"

"Don't talk to the suspects," Tansy said in my ear. "He didn't say *I* couldn't though."

Sure enough, I found several of the Sky Hopper team members waiting in the small room, sitting on uncomfortable-looking metal chairs. The two female Vultures I'd spoken to at the party, Gwen and Everly, sat on one side of the room. Opposite them sat a lanky redheaded man with a bandage wrapped around his head whose name I vaguely remembered as Tomas, who'd been unfortunate enough to get knocked out during their last game.

I took an unoccupied chair next to the younger Vulture with the chipped tooth and lasted approximately ten seconds before Everly broke the silence. "Hey, Robin. I thought you already gave your statement."

I shrugged, unable to avoid noticing when everyone's gazes darted in my direction. "Nah, I haven't. How long have you been here?"

"Since this morning," put in Gwen, the older Vulture. "The police asked all the team members to come back to give their statements first, since there were too many people to question at once."

"So… is Harvey here?"

"He's giving his statement right now," Gwen replied. "So is Cole."

My heart flipped over. It'd have been nice if Ramsey had told *me* that Harvey was being questioned right this instant. "Did Gabriel already speak to them?" I'd assumed that must be the case, since I'd seen him in the coffee shop earlier.

At the mention of Gabriel's name, the bandaged man gave a twitch as if trying to shake off a fly that had landed on his shoulder. When I glanced in his direction, his jaw tensed, and he looked away.

"Yeah," answered Everly. "Poor kid didn't expect the guy he's replacing to end up being murdered at his own leaving party."

"I bet," I murmured. "Do the police think someone on the team was the culprit?"

Disgust rippled across Gwen's face. "I don't believe it. Not for a second. We look out for one another, all of us. Jansen was the best of us."

Who did it then? The killer had used the captain's badge to commit murder, not to mention killing Jansen in as public a manner as possible in front of all the team's fans. They'd wanted to make a spectacle, but I had the sneaking suspicion that sowing discord amid the players might have also been the intention.

"This takes fighting dirty to a whole new level," I remarked. "Did Jansen have any rivals? I don't know, like players he's defeated in past matches who might hold a grudge?"

"Too many to count, considering how long he was on the team," Everly replied. "But I don't see any of them murdering him at his own leaving party. He's no longer in the game, after all, and besides, the pub was full of our own supporters."

Again, Tomas twitched in his seat, his gaze darting around the room without resting on any spot in particular.

I fidgeted, wondering if it would be unsporting to ask him what he found so objectionable about our discussion. "What about his life outside the sport then?"

"Not sure he had one," Gwen commented. "He was married once... didn't last."

"Jansen was always utterly devoted to the game," added Everly. "Any long-term relationship would have had to settle for second place."

Hmm. "Was there anyone he didn't get along with? Inside or outside of the game? Or anyone he argued with recently?"

"He had a strong personality," said Gwen. "When he was captain, he tended to dig his heels in whenever someone argued with an idea he thought was right. That wasn't recent though."

"He was never unfair to anyone," Everly added. "And even after Harvey took over as captain, he was always ready to answer questions, even offer mentoring to anyone who was struggling."

I debated asking what they thought of Harvey taking his place, but that would be way out of the scope of the investigation and more to satisfy my personal curiosity. Besides, Harvey had become captain long before Jansen's murder.

The waiting room door opened, and one of Ramsey's fellow police officers called Tomas in for questioning. The bandaged man rose to his feet unsteadily, as if he was either still drunk or injured. When he left the room to give his statement, he walked into a metal chair on the way, causing a resounding *clunk* to echo throughout the room.

"What's up with him?" I whispered to the others. "Did he fall off his broom?"

"Yeah, and broke three ribs," said Everly in a low voice. "He shouldn't be walking around if you ask me."

Gwen made a sceptical noise. "He's the one who refused to go to the hospital because he wanted to go out drinking instead. Waste of time, since he spent the whole night ignoring all of us."

I recalled seeing him sulking at the bar while everyone else had been celebrating. Hardly sporting, but he probably shouldn't have been at the party to begin with if he'd recently fallen off his broomstick.

Before the door closed behind Tomas, I glimpsed Harvey walking past. My heart flipped over in my chest, and when he caught sight of me, his eyes widened. I crossed the room and caught the door in my hand.

"Hey." I stood in the doorway, conscious that the others were no doubt listening in from the waiting room, and spoke in a low voice. "I thought you were giving your statement."

"I did," he replied. "What are you doing here?"

"Same as you." I might have added more if we hadn't had an audience, but at that moment, Ramsey appeared behind him like an apparition, levelling his sternest expression at both of us.

"Robin, sit down," he ordered. "Harvey, aren't you supposed to be leaving?"

Harvey rotated to face my brother. "My apologies. I wanted to check on my team, but I didn't realise Robin would be here."

Ramsey's lips compressed. Harvey had been perfectly polite, so my brother would have a hard time finding a reason to fault his behaviour. "Robin is here to give her own perspective on the events of last night. Your team is fine. Go on, leave."

I mouthed *Sorry* at Harvey as he departed, and he shot me an apologetic look in return.

Ramsey didn't budge from the doorway. "Now's as good a time as any for you to come and give your statement, Robin."

He wanted me to give the statement to *him?* So much for being treated the same as the others, though I'd already drawn unwanted attention by speaking to Harvey to begin with. Ah, well. The sooner I got this over with, the sooner I'd be able to talk to Harvey face-to-face.

Ramsey beckoned me across the lobby. "Let's get this over with."

"I thought you wanted my help," I said out of the corner of my mouth as Tansy and I followed him through the lobby to his office.

He pushed open the door. "I didn't ask you to start chatting to every team member in the waiting room. I distinctly recall telling you to do the opposite, in fact."

"I wasn't offering them tips on getting away with murder, Ramsey." I entered the small office, Tansy scampering ahead of me and onto my brother's desk. "I was trying to find out why someone on the Sky Hopper team would bump off their own former captain. So far, most of them seem to think it wasn't a team member responsible at all."

"The verdict will speak for itself." He stepped behind his desk and snatched a handful of papers out of the path of Tansy's fluffy tail before sitting down. "Robin, tell me what you saw in the moments leading up to Jansen's death."

Straight to the point then. I perched on the chair opposite his and cast a look around the office—impeccably tidy as always, and in stark contrast to the office I'd inherited from my grandmother. "From which moment, exactly? I can start at the beginning of the party, but frankly, I don't remember every single person I was introduced to."

"Tell me what you do remember."

"I arrived at the pub and met the rest of the team," I began. "They liked Tansy."

My familiar hopped onto the arm of my chair. "Of course they did. I'm extremely likeable."

Unimpressed, Ramsey went on. "Then?"

"Someone brought out the cake," I recalled. "The team wanted Jansen to cut it himself, which he did. He took the first slice, and when they were passing plates around, he started choking and died."

"Did you see anyone put anything on his plate?"

"No, I didn't, but I wasn't looking," I admitted. "They might have done it in the kitchen instead… but I suppose they'd have had to know exactly which slice he'd take. Do you know who made the cake?"

"The cake was custom-made at the local bakery," Ramsey said. "Nobody there was known to the team, and the badge was intentionally put into his slice at some point between it leaving the bakery and the moment of Jansen's death. That's all I've been able to deduce so far."

I turned this over in my head. "There were so many people in the pub that it's certainly possible for someone to have slipped it into his slice without being seen while it was on its way across the room. There must have been easily a hundred people in there, and anyone with a sneaky enough hand might have been responsible."

"No doubt that's exactly why the killer picked their moment," he said. "That said, it seems more likely that one of the people sitting close to Jansen himself put the badge in there, to ensure it reached the right target."

"You mean the rest of the team," I surmised. "Though everyone crowded around to watch him cut the cake, so it wasn't necessarily a team member who did it."

"Are you positive you didn't spot anything that struck

you as out of place?" he asked. "Did anyone leave the party immediately after the cake was cut?"

"You think the killer did a runner?" I considered this. "Unlikely. The crowd was pretty thick, and since everyone was wearing red, it was hard to tell if anyone wasn't supposed to be there."

"Inconvenient," he muttered. "The others all said the same."

"I doubt you're going to get anything useful from listening to a dozen accounts of the same events," I told him. "It'd save you a lot of time if you skipped straight to questioning people who might have a motive to kill Jansen."

"That was my intention with questioning the team members," he said. "In my experience, it's often someone close to the victim who is responsible, and by all accounts, Jansen had few interests outside of his team."

Talk about the pot calling the kettle black, considering that Ramsey was married to his job. "He was married once, apparently."

"I'm already looking into that." He rose to his feet. "That's all, Robin. I'll let you know if we come to any conclusions."

"You mean if you arrest someone." I stood, and Tansy scampered up my side to my shoulder. "Ramsey, I'm not going to tell the entire town if you give me the details on who you suspect. I might be able to help you."

"You already told Rowan and Piper."

Ah. He'd correctly guessed the reason for our morning gathering in the café. "They won't spread it around either. They were a lot of help with solving Grandma's murder…"

"Don't even go there, Robin." He pressed a hand to his forehead. "The circumstances were entirely different. The Head Witch's murder was the business of the entire coven by necessity. This, however, is a matter for the police to solve and nobody else."

I tilted my head. "What if it turned out that the assassin was trying to target me and got the wrong person again? Would it be my business then?"

Tansy snorted. "Come on, Robin. You don't seriously think an assassin would try to choke you to death on the Sky Hopper captain's badge, do you?"

"Hey, it's a valid strategy." And an excuse for me to lend a hand. I wouldn't stoop to using my Head Witch status to muscle in on the investigation, but Ramsey had already admitted—reluctantly—that I'd been helpful in his last major investigation. The fact that I'd turned out to be the intended target was neither here nor there.

Ramsey looked unimpressed. "If it's true, then it's even more of a reason to stay away from my suspects."

"Not when they aren't at the police station." Over my dead body was I going to avoid Harvey until the case was resolved. "Relax. If I don't accept any cake from anyone, then I'll be fine."

"It's not that simple, and you know it."

I had an inkling I was fighting a losing battle by arguing with him, but I refused to let this murder case prevent me from seeing Harvey again. He *wasn't* the killer, nor was he close to a suspect—whatever my brother might claim.

"I'll refrain from striking up conversations in the waiting room, but the coffee shop is another matter. Deal?"

His jaw twitched. "Fine."

"Excellent." I took a step towards the door. "My offer of help is open if you change your mind."

Ramsey said nothing while Tansy and I left his office and then walked out of the police station. I pulled out my phone on the walk to Were's My Coffee?, finding a message from Piper saying she still had a bit of a headache, so she'd gone home.

It was nearly lunchtime, so I returned to the café alone and found Rowan still at work on her shift. She shot me a smile when I reached the front of the queue. "There you are. I was beginning to wonder if your brother had cracked and locked you in a cell to stop you from badgering him."

"Nah, he just let me give a statement and stuck to the rulebook." I pulled a face. "As opposed to actually letting me help him with the investigation. He kicked up a fuss about me talking to the other team members."

"Not Harvey?" She swore under her breath. "He's not going to go as far as to stop you from seeing him… is he?"

"I bloody hope not." I grimaced. "I don't get the impression Ramsey likes him very much, probably because Harvey *does* like me. Mum already gave me a lecture about how he's not a suitable romantic partner for a Head Witch, and I wouldn't be surprised if she'd told Ramsey the same."

"Honestly." She shook her head. "You can make your own decisions. You told me that, remember?"

"That was true… before I became Head Witch." I lowered my gaze. "According to my family, I have forfeited all choice over my romantic prospects until I give up the sceptre. Since I don't know when that'll be and neither does anyone else, they've decided to keep acting as if I'm either a nun or secretly betrothed to someone who doesn't exist."

She snorted. "As if your mother never dated before she met your dad."

"She wasn't Head Witch at the time though," I pointed out. "Also, it's not just being Head Witch that's the issue. It's the fact that I'm inexperienced at the job, and I'm also the target of potential assassins everywhere I go."

"There is that," said Rowan. "He's not going to *arrest* Harvey, is he?"

"I hope not." I gave a shudder. "It's more likely that he'll use it as an excuse to keep us from spending time together."

"Siblings." She rolled her eyes. "Anyway, can I get you anything?"

"A sandwich, please. No lattes. I've had enough caffeine today already." I needed a long walk to get rid of the excess energy, but what I really wanted was to see Harvey. Romantic interest aside, he was the team captain and was no doubt going through a tough time as a result of Jansen's death. He hadn't deserved to spend the morning dealing with the police's suspicions after losing a friend and mentor.

I paid for my sandwich and returned to my regular table to eat it, wondering if the quickest way to get Ramsey to see sense was to bite my tongue and wait for him to come to the decision on his own. I'd really thought we'd begun to make progress when I'd helped find the person who'd killed two of the contenders at the familiar contest a few weeks ago, but my proximity to Jansen's death must have brought my brother's overprotective tendencies out in full force.

My phone buzzed with a message from Harvey asking if I wanted to meet up. *Aha.* I was glad that he wouldn't be easily put off by my brother's attitude.

Hiding a grin, I replied, saying yes. Never mind playing by my brother's rules. I'd do this my way.

5

Harvey and I met up in a shaded stretch of the woodland trail, which cut through the forested area on the northern side of town and circled the row of houses that belonged to the major coven families from behind. Out of anyone's sight, I was reasonably confident that nobody would spot us unless they decided to take a long walk in the forest. After all, there was a good reason I'd picked this particular route as the ideal place to escape my family when I'd lived at home full-time.

Harvey himself looked quite relieved to be away from the police's attention. When he smiled at me, my heart gave another flip. Despite the dark circles under his eyes and the stubble on his face, since he'd had no time to shave that morning, he looked particularly handsome today.

"Hey, Robin. Sorry about earlier."

I shook my head. "I should be apologising to you instead. My brother's attitude leaves much to be desired."

"It's no big deal," he said. "He was only doing his job."

"He could stand to be a little more pleasant when he isn't interrogating people." I fell into step with him on the woodland trail. "You gave your statement, right?"

"I did, yes," he replied. "I don't expect it to be my last though. I'm the captain of the team, after all, so it's only natural that the police would have more questions for me. Besides, I'm obligated to take responsibility for the others."

Not if one of them is a murderer. I held back from voicing that particular thought aloud and instead said, "Might take them a while to get through questioning all the guests from the party though. Not to mention everyone else who was at the pub last night."

"I thought so." He was silent for a moment. "Ramsey didn't give you a hard time, did he?"

"No." Wasn't I supposed to be asking him that question instead of the other way around? "I'm not the one on the suspect list. Not that you're in danger of being arrested or anything…" *I hope.*

"He's under stress, which I completely understand."

"So are you," I pointed out. "He *did* tell me off for talking to your teammates in the waiting room, but I made it clear that he can't stop me from speaking to any of you outside of the police station. That's not within the limits of his job description."

"Good." His mouth tilted up at the corner. "I never anticipated that I might have to break the law to get a date with you."

A flash of red caught my eye as Tansy ascended a tree and vanished from sight, leaving the pair of us alone together. Meanwhile, warmth spread in my chest despite the knowledge that the universe had thoroughly thwarted any hopes of us getting said date without Ramsey's interference.

"Nah, it's not the law that's the problem. My brother… I think part of him is convinced that he's still fifteen and I'm twelve."

"I get it," he said. "I have two little brothers of my own."

My lips parted. "I forgot."

I shouldn't have, since Harvey and I had been in the same class at the academy as kids, but that had been a long time ago. A lot had changed since those days. If we'd had an actual date, we might have been able to catch up on the missing years in between, but instead, our rekindling of our friendship had consisted of a string of clandestine meetings, often interrupted, thanks to my sudden and inconvenient ascension to the position of Head Witch.

He exhaled. "My next move was to ask if you'd like to go to the Fox's Den *without* the rest of the team, but I can't imagine it's going to seem an appealing site for a date until the murder is solved."

"No kidding." I might have hoped *this* could be a date of sorts, but he'd been in interrogation all morning and clearly just wanted to talk to someone. That he'd picked me was reason enough to be glad my brother hadn't thoroughly scuppered our chances, at least. "I offered to help my brother with the investigation, but he seems to think I can't be trusted to keep my mouth shut."

"You *did* help to find the murderer at the familiar contest," he pointed out. "Not to mention your grandmother's killer."

"Yeah, but he suddenly took exception to my discussing the details with Rowan and Piper." I gave an eye roll. "And you, but he doesn't have to know we're talking about the case."

"I guess it's probably frowned upon to talk about the case with someone who's technically a suspect…"

"You're not a suspect," I said firmly. "Have you spoken to the rest of the team since last night?"

"Not much, except to offer my condolences and to reassure them that the killer will be brought to justice," he replied. "I don't know what we're going to do about team practise next week though."

"When's your next session scheduled?"

"Monday," he replied. "It'll be Gabriel's first full session with the rest of the team, too, which isn't ideal for any of us."

"Speaking of whom, Ramsey scared the hell out of Gabriel earlier when I was talking to him in the coffee shop," I said. "Poor guy. He seems to think he'll take the blame for this."

"He won't," said Harvey. "Or rather, he shouldn't."

I thought back to the little I knew of the shy newcomer. "He said the team voted him in as a replacement, but it sounds like he was surprised to get picked. Was it Jansen who made the final call?"

Harvey inclined his head. "And me, but I let Jansen make the decision, since he was the one Gabriel was going to be replacing. Gabriel's a good player. Not as good as Jansen, true, but he's young enough that he has time to develop his technique. Once he's gone through a few games with the other players, he'll be ready for the big leagues, I've no doubt."

"How long has Jansen been planning to retire?" I asked. "He stepped down as captain before he left the team, so I'm guessing he didn't want to step aside."

"Got it in one," he said. "It's not that uncommon, but we've spent years trying to convince him to stay on as a consultant rather than constantly risking injury in the air. We had the same conversation at least once a week, and he was usually the person I went to for a second opinion on anything."

A pang hit me. It'd slipped my mind that Harvey had had no time to mourn his teammate and friend, what with having to take full responsibility for the rest of the players as well as dealing with interrogations from the police.

"Sorry," I murmured. "I should have remembered... I mean, I know you must have been close."

"Yeah... it's going to be weird without him around." He wore a pensive expression as we continued to walk along the woodland path. "Some of the other team members thought he stayed far past the time when he should have retired, but they liked having him around enough that it didn't matter. We'll all miss him."

I didn't doubt that. As little as I wanted to poke around by asking questions on a sore subject, I knew it would be a great help if the killer was found as quickly as possible so that the team could return to mourning their friend in peace.

"Anyway," he went on, "he wouldn't want us to get caught up in mourning him when there are games to be won. That's why I'm going ahead with Monday's practise session. He'd want us to try our best, and he'd definitely want our newest player to be prepared for our next major match."

"When exactly did Gabriel get picked for the team?" I asked.

"Before yesterday's game," he said. "Jansen announced his retirement a week ago, and we opened up applications to anyone who was interested, but we only made the announcement to the rest of the team when we were getting ready for Jansen's final match."

Yesterday? If that was the reason for Jansen's death, then the killer must have acted quickly when they'd thrown their plan together. Perhaps that was why they'd had him choke to death on a badge rather than a subtler approach like poisoning the cake, since it would doubtless have already been prepared.

"Were there other people who wanted to be Jansen's replacement and were annoyed that Gabriel was chosen instead?" I asked Harvey. "Or was it a pretty unanimous decision?"

"Plenty of others *wanted* to join the team," he answered. "We had several rounds of trials, narrowed it down to the best handful, and then picked the best from among them. I let the rest of the team know he won right before our match."

"So he hasn't had the chance to practise with any of the other players?"

"No." His mouth turned down at the corners. "Maybe I rushed into the decision, but Jansen was adamant about playing in our last game, and we wanted to hold the party afterwards."

"Were any of the people who failed the tryouts at the party?" I asked curiously.

"Of course," he answered. "They were team supporters, and I didn't get the sense of any hard feelings. Granted, I was paying more attention to the team, not the hundred or so other people who showed up."

Except for me, but I hadn't been paying any attention either. The pub had been too crowded, and with every person in the room dressed in red, an outsider would have stuck out like a sore thumb. "Is that more likely than someone on the team itself being responsible?"

His expression shadowed. "I hate to even think about any of my fellow team members doing such a thing, but I'm not going to accuse a stranger either. I told your brother as much."

"Good." I took the lead around the corner where the woodland path looped back on itself. "I don't have any theories, either, except that some of your team probably weren't in a fit state for questioning this morning. Tomas, for one."

"Tomas?" he echoed. "Right—he fell off his broom and got himself a concussion yesterday. Refused to check into the hospital either, but nobody wanted to miss the party."

"He didn't look much like he was celebrating," I remarked. "I imagine those injuries are common enough with Vultures though."

"There's a reason I never tried out for that position," he said. "I prefer supporting my own team to haranguing our opponents, personally."

"Especially with the injury risk." Yet I couldn't shake the feeling that more than a concussion had affected Tomas's attitude. The dirty look he'd given Gabriel at the party and the way he'd twitched when I'd mentioned his name in the waiting room had caught my eye. He plainly didn't like the newcomer, but that didn't mean the same had been true of the former captain.

"Exactly."

As we followed the looping path, I thought back to my conversation with the Vultures at the police station. "I talked to some of the other team members, and one of them mentioned that the former captain had a strong personality. Did he often argue with the others?"

"Not at all," he said. "He was always fair. Unless someone went out of their way to give him trouble, he didn't go out of his way to impose on anyone. He wanted the whole team to get along well, since we played best when everyone was comfortable with one another."

"I just wondered if someone's been harbouring a long-festering grudge or something."

"Not that I'm aware of." He paused. "One person did leave the team a year or two ago, but it wasn't to do with Jansen, I don't think. It happened before I got promoted to captain."

"You've only been captain for a year?"

"Nine months," he said. "Give or take a week or two."

"Ah." Jansen hadn't stepped down long ago, not at all. "Anyway, you said someone quit the team. Who?"

"You won't know him," he said. "Casey… he was kind of a hothead from what I remember. Never much of a team player. I think most people were relieved when he quit."

"Was he at the party?"

"Not that I saw, but there were a lot of people around," he said. "He still lives in Wildwood Heath though, so I expect his name will come up at some point if they don't find the culprit soon. I guess I could have mentioned him to the police, but they have enough people to question already."

"Yeah, a hundred or so witnesses, including the two of us," I commented. "You'd think Ramsey would leap at the chance to hand some of the work over to me instead, but the guy has no concept of delegation."

"I thought the two of you were getting along better," he said. "After the contest, I mean."

"We were. I don't know what his problem is." Except with my romantic choices, that is, but over my dead body was I telling him *that*. Or that my mother had opinions on who the Head Witch would be suited to pursue a relationship with, either, for that matter. "I know he's the leader of the police as well as my brother, but he doesn't have authority over me."

"Good." His expression relaxed. "I'd hate for our friendship to be another casualty of this sorry mess."

Friendship. I'd rather hoped he might say something else instead, but discussing a murder was kind of a mood killer. "Same, but it won't be. If Ramsey tries to kick up a fuss, then Tansy and I have a list of ways we can annoy him into submission."

"You can't use your authority as Head Witch?"

I winced. "Technically? Yes. But in the interests of keeping the peace, I'd rather not."

"I didn't mean to make you uncomfortable," he said. "Sorry. I know it's probably a risk to your reputation to be seen talking to a murder suspect as well—"

"Please don't talk to me about reputations," I interjected. "I want to help you."

More than that: I wanted to keep seeing him, investigation or not.

He smiled. "I appreciate it."

My heart fluttered in my chest. "You know, when you said *friendship*—"

A flash of red caught my eye, and Tansy came sliding down a tree branch to land in front of me. "It might interest you to know that your mother is walking down the woodland trail. I think she's looking for you."

I stifled a groan. "How does she even know I'm out here?"

She didn't, surely, but that would change if she saw me with Harvey. I turned back to him, and he gave me a questioning look. "You're going home?"

"Definitely not, but I suppose now's as good a time as any to pay a visit to my dad." The one place where Mum was guaranteed not to follow me. Ramsey too. "I'll see you later?"

"Sure." He flashed me another smile, but he didn't move any closer. Probably because Tansy had just jumped onto my shoulder and was waving her tail in my face, urging me to get a move on. "I'll text you."

He departed, while I made my way towards my dad's cottage at the far end of the woodland trail. Tansy bounded off my shoulder, and I rolled my eyes at her. "You didn't have to be that insistent."

"If you two had ended up making out in the bushes, you'd have got caught."

"We're not teenagers."

"Could have fooled me." Tansy scampered alongside my heels. "I thought you were going to help solve the murder."

"We *were* talking about the murder," I pointed out. "Do you have any theories on the killer's identity?"

"Your guess is as good as mine," she replied. "I know

Harvey doesn't want to consider the possibility of anyone on the team being the killer, but they knew Jansen best, didn't they?"

"I guess they did." That was the problem. "Ramsey said it's likely to be someone who was close to Jansen too."

If not for my desire to help Harvey and the lingering guilt over witnessing Jansen's death without being able to offer any substantial information of my own, I'd have been more than happy to leave the investigating to Ramsey. As it was though, I couldn't imagine turning my back. My brother would just have to deal with it.

I came to a halt where the woodland trail ended at my dad's house. The pleasant cottage was a fraction of the size of my family's home but much more cosy looking, with ivy growing on the whitewashed walls and the sound of hyperactive werewolf kids playing in the garden in the background. Jessica's two kids, Jake and Spike, must have been at home and enjoying the pleasant weather.

Dad answered my knock on the door with a grin and a hug. "I wondered when you'd drop by. Busy week?"

"Yeah, but manageable. Mostly."

I assumed he hadn't heard about the investigation, since he and Ramsey weren't on speaking terms. Not for a lack of effort on Dad's part or mine, but Ramsey's capacity to hold a grudge was rivalled only by his dedication to his policing career.

"Good." He invited me into the living room. "I'm glad you're settling back in."

I picked out a seat among the piles of toys, while Tansy scampered onto the windowsill to watch the tumbling werewolves outside. I grinned at the sight of Jessica in her werewolf form chasing her two kids around the garden.

Dad might not have been a werewolf himself, but he had no objection to the young wolves' raucous behaviour—a welcome contrast to certain other family members of mine.

"Sort of." I assumed he didn't want to hear about the trials and tribulations of being Head Witch, and besides, I wanted to avoid the subject for a bit. Instead, I asked the usual questions about the kids and work and did my best to avoid mentioning the rest of the family.

"At least they let you take weekends off," he remarked. "Did you do anything fun last night?"

The inevitable question brought a moment's debate on whether I should sidestep yesterday's events, but I figured he'd rather hear it from me. "I went to a party at the pub yesterday with the Sky Hopper team. Harvey invited me."

"That's great news." Unlike my mother, he didn't give a crap who I dated and actively encouraged my social life. "How'd it go?"

"Great until the guy who the party was being hosted for choked to death, and now my brother is spearheading the murder investigation."

"You're joking," he said. "No, you're not. Oh, no."

"Relax, Dad. I wasn't the target this time."

"I'm glad of that, at least." He shook his head. "There's always something, isn't there?"

"Tell me about it." I heaved a sigh. "I want to help the Sky Hopper team find out who was responsible, especially Harvey, but Ramsey is getting all touchy about me offering my assistance."

"I can imagine." Dad knew better than most people how stubborn my brother could be, considering that after our parents had divorced, Ramsey had gone years without exchanging more than a few words at a time with our father. He'd be equally willing to go to any lengths to stop me from involving myself in a murder investigation, even one involving my would-be boyfriend, and by Ramsey's usual standards, he'd been positively restrained so far.

I watched the werewolves wrestling one another for a moment. "That's my life. Be glad you only have to deal with getting werewolf fur out of the carpets."

"Hey, nobody's perfect," Dad said. "Not even that uptight brother of yours. Keep trying. You'll wear him down."

I gave him a considering look. "I'll try."

6

---

arvey sent me a message the following morning asking if I wanted to meet up at Were's My Coffee? I said yes right away and left the house before anyone else could come downstairs and waylay me on my way out. After our walk in the forest had abruptly been cut short the previous day, I wanted to check in with Harvey and see if I could shed any light on the murderer.

"Or make out with him," Tansy replied when I said this aloud.

"I seem to remember a squirrel falling on my face last time I tried." Actually, I'd been trying to find out what he'd meant when he'd mentioned our friendship, though maybe that wasn't all there was to it. You could be friends *and* romantic partners, right? It didn't have to be one or the other.

Ramsey hadn't returned from the office until late the previous evening. I hoped my ridiculous brother was actually getting some sleep at the moment, because at this rate, the investigation would drag on for days, if not weeks. Since he hadn't deigned to give me an update on his progress, I made a mental note to ask Harvey if he'd been called back to be questioned again.

As I reached Were's My Coffee?, a magpie took flight from the gutter above my head and brought me to a halt. "Was that Myrtle?"

"I'll have a look," Tansy replied, scaling the drainpipe. "You go and meet Harvey. He's already waiting for you."

That had better not be Aunt Shannon's familiar. Unsettled, I walked into the café and found Harvey already sitting at a table. Rowan wasn't working today, and since she wasn't downstairs, maybe she'd stayed in her room to play video games. Not a terrible idea, though her mother's familiar had better not be spying on her when she wasn't paying attention.

After ordering my usual latte, I joined Harvey. "Hey."

He smiled at me, and I found myself smiling in response despite my lingering unease. "Hey, Robin. Where's Tansy?"

"Looking for magpies." I sat down opposite him. "Or one magpie in particular. My aunt's familiar."

"Why would she be... oh, no."

"Yeah." I lowered my voice. "If Aunt Shannon is trying to spy on her daughter, then using her familiar is her go-to strategy."

We both looked out the window, seeing no magpies. When a man with dark hair and a leather jacket walked past, Harvey's gaze followed him. "Casey... I wonder if the police got in touch with him after all."

"Who?" I frowned. "Casey... wait, the guy who left the Sky Hopper team before you were captain?"

"Exactly." Harvey rose to his feet. "I'll find out if he spoke to them yet."

I did likewise before I could think better of it and followed him to the door. Harvey's long-legged stride caught up to the man first. "Hey—Casey."

"What do *you* want?" Casey didn't stop walking, forcing Harvey to quicken his pace, while I lagged behind both of them.

"To talk," Harvey replied. "Did the police call you in for questioning?"

"So that was your doing, was it?" growled Casey. "I should have known."

"No need to be rude," I told him. "What's the problem?"

"Him." He finally came to a halt, giving Harvey a blistering look.

"I can see that." I folded my arms. "He wants to talk to you, nothing more. You could stand to be a little nicer to your former teammate."

"I didn't mention your name to the police, Casey," Harvey ventured. "I wasn't aware they were questioning anyone outside the team yet."

"Oh, believe me, they are," said Casey in sour tones. "Since nobody wants to admit there's a killer on their own team."

What? "And you know all about the investigation, do you?"

His gaze slid to me. "Do *you* know anything?"

"My brother is the chief of police," I informed him. "So yes, I'm aware of the investigation into the death of the former captain, as well as his list of suspects."

He studied my face. "You're the Head Witch, aren't you?"

"Yes, but that's irrelevant," I said smoothly. "What isn't irrelevant is that I was at the party myself, and I saw Jansen's death. Were *you?*"

"No, I most certainly wasn't," he responded. "I was at work. Now, quit badgering me, both of you."

He walked away. I watched him for a moment and then raised a brow at Harvey. "Is he always like this?"

"Only around former team members," he replied. "His alibi will be easy enough to verify. I happen to know he works at the Mermaid's Meadow."

"Seriously?" The guy looked more like he belonged in a grungy motorcycle shop than a nightclub, but I couldn't picture him on a broomstick either. Harvey's remark that he hadn't been a team player seemed accurate though. "I'd tell my brother, but I think he's asleep."

"You don't have to tell him," he said. "In fact, it's probably better if you don't. The police will contact Casey themselves if they think he knows anything."

We returned to the café, where I belatedly remembered that Tansy still hadn't come back from her hunt for Myrtle the magpie. Maybe she'd got distracted chasing the local pigeons around. "I can see why Casey quit the team with that attitude of his."

His mouth turned down at the corners. "It didn't use to be like that. I can't imagine him doing anything to Jansen though. If anything, he got on better with the old captain than anyone else on the team."

I sat down at the table opposite him. "I guess the police want to cover all their bases. Anyone else you want to grab for questioning?"

"Better keep that to a minimum," he replied. "Though now that you mention it, tomorrow evening is our first practise session with Gabriel on our team."

"You don't think my brother will kick up a fuss, do you?" I asked. "He doesn't really get Sky Hopper or how hard you guys work. I can try to explain to him if you like."

"You don't have to," he said. "But I wondered if you wanted to come and watch?"

"Really?" My voice rose in surprise. "Are you sure?"

"It's all right if not," he added. "I just thought that if the Head Witch is watching the practise session, the police shouldn't have an issue."

Except for my brother, but he had a point there. "I bet the killer will think twice about trying anything funny with the Head Witch supervising your practise session. What time?"

"Tomorrow evening at six," he said. "We usually practise at the sports ground near the academy, which is reachable from the woodland path."

Perfect: I could get there without running into certain family members. "Sure, I'll be there."

"Good," he said. "I know it's not ideal, but if we finish early, I can take you to dinner. Not at the Fox's Den though."

My heart backflipped. "Pity. I love that place."

He smiled. "Maybe we can get away with it. We'll see."

"Of course." My Monday suddenly looked a whole lot brighter. "See you tomorrow."

———

"Where have you been?" Ramsey grouched at me as I entered the house.

"Getting coffee. Have you seen Tansy?" She'd been gone for a couple of hours by now, and when I peered through the back window at the garden, I didn't see her terrorising the local pigeons either.

"Lost her, did you?" Prickles sat across from a bowl of milk on the kitchen table. "I didn't know Rowan was an early riser."

"It's not that early," I evaded, opting not to mention that it hadn't been Rowan I'd met with. "Also, shouldn't you be asleep, Ramsey?"

"I have to go back into the office." He looked almost dishevelled, compared to his usual self, with his shirt untucked and his hair rumpled. "To check in with my colleagues."

"Speaking of whom," I said, unable to help myself, "which of them questioned Casey, the ex-Sky Hopper team member?"

"Who told you that?"

I probably should have come up with a plausible cover story first. "I ran into him near the café…"

"Harvey told you, didn't he?" His eyes narrowed. "You met him at the café."

Should have seen that one coming. "We weren't anywhere near the police station, so don't get your broomstick in a tangle. He recognised Casey and asked him if he'd been questioned…"

"He shouldn't have done that."

"You can't stop Harvey from talking to his teammates, Ramsey," I pointed out. "Or ex-teammates, as it were. It might interest you to know that Casey claimed that he was at work at the Mermaid's Meadow nightclub during the party, if you want to check his alibi."

"What?" He reached for his mobile phone, possibly to input that information. "You're not supposed to be asking my suspects questions, Robin."

"I offered to help wherever I could." He didn't need to act as if I'd marched into his office and started rearranging his desk. "I'm not trying to make your life harder; quite the opposite."

Prickles made a sceptical noise. "I don't think you know the difference."

"Oi." Doubly annoyed, I gave up all pretence at diplomacy. "I'll be out of your hair all day tomorrow, don't worry. After work, I'm going to watch the Sky Hopper team's practise session, so I'll let you know if anyone acts out of line."

Ramsey nearly dropped his phone. "You let him invite you to watch the team practise?"

"*Let* him?" I echoed. "I'm not a Seer, Ramsey. I hardly knew he planned to invite me, but it's after I'm done with work, so it won't get in the way of my schedule."

"That isn't the issue," he said. "Robin, you have no reason whatsoever to be there and several reasons *not* to be anywhere near the Sky Hopper team. Not least because Jansen's murder isn't resolved yet. Frankly, they shouldn't be meeting up at all."

"They need to practise, Ramsey," I said. "Gabriel hasn't joined in a team practise session yet, and they have a match coming up in a couple of weeks. Besides, if none of them has actually been arrested, then you can't prevent them from meeting up."

I might have added in another comment or two about

his complete lack of understanding of Sky Hopper and how much work it required, but I managed to refrain, even though dealing with my brother when he was in one of these moods was like handling Prickles with my bare hands.

"I can't stop their practise session," he allowed. "I just don't think *you* should be there."

Here we go again. "Members of the public are allowed to spectate. I'm not violating any rules by being there."

"There's a good chance you might be in close proximity to the murderer, Robin. That is what concerns me."

"I'm not the murderer's target, Ramsey. Besides, there also won't be any cake this time." When he glowered at me, I added, "I'll take the sceptre with me then. Happy?"

"I thought you hadn't mastered its magic yet."

Had Grandma been telling tales on me? "I don't have a problem using its magic to defend myself, and if I end up toe-to-toe with a killer, moderation is the last thing I'll need."

"That doesn't mean our mother will be as easily convinced if she finds out."

"Depends if you tell her." Though there was an equal chance that she might spot me leaving the office and demand to know where I was going—or ambush me when I came back. "It'd cut your investigation short if I walloped the killer on the head with my sceptre, you know."

"That's highly unlikely." Ramsey beckoned to Prickles, who hopped off the table to join his owner. "I'm not going to argue with you any longer, Robin. It's your risk to take."

The pair of them left the room while I shook my head after them. Some people questioned how my brother had ended up with a hedgehog as a familiar, but even if you discounted Prickles's own personality, his spiky exterior summed up Ramsey's in a nutshell. Granted, somewhere underneath all the spikes was the brother who'd had my back since day one, which was easy to forget when we were trading blows.

As the front door closed behind my brother, Tansy came limping into the room, her tail dragging behind her.

"There you are." I ran to my familiar's side. "What did you do? Fall off the bird feeder?"

"I never *fall*," she said with a great deal of dignity. "Nor do I trip."

"You're hurt." Suspicion hit me. "Was it Myrtle?"

She groaned and flopped onto her back, her paws sticking up in the air. "My feet hurt."

Alarmed, I crouched at her side. "What did she do to you?"

"Not *she, it*," she said. "Someone put a *net* in the forest. I barely got out of there with my tail intact."

Now that I looked closer, her feet were covered in a sticky substance that bound her little paws together. It was a wonder she'd even managed to limp home.

"What is this?" I prodded the edge, which stuck to my fingertips like glue. "A giant spiderweb?"

"Something like that." Tansy yelped when I tugged at the piece of thread. "Ow."

"Hang on." I half rose to my feet then realised I didn't know if Mum had moved the cabinet of our ingredients and first-aid supplies in the years since I'd been gone. "We can drop by the apothecary to see if they have anything to remove it. Or I'll ask Rowan. She's the expert on spiderwebs out of the two of us."

If Myrtle had been lurking outside the shop as well as leading Tansy into a trap, then Rowan would want to know. While she wouldn't be thrilled when I mentioned that her scheming mother might still be trying to interfere in her life, it was better for her to know the truth than be taken by surprise.

"All right." Tansy groaned when I gingerly picked her up, cradling her in my arms.

Her behaviour was out of character to say the least, and it lit a flame of anger inside me to think that someone had had the nerve to hurt my familiar.

I fired off a text message to Rowan and then left the house with Tansy in my arms. When I reached the café, Rowan messaged me with instructions on how to get to the upper floor where she lived. I ducked down the narrow alleyway between the café and the neighbouring building and then rang the doorbell to the upstairs flat.

Rowan's face appeared in the upstairs window, and she mouthed, "Just a second."

A few moments later, the back door clicked open, revealing Rowan standing at the foot of a narrow stairway. "Hey, Robin… what's wrong with Tansy?"

"She ran into some kind of trap in the forest," I replied. "Like a giant spiderweb. Can you help me get this off? I think it's hurting her."

"Sure thing." She headed up the creaky staircase, while I carried Tansy behind her.

A short corridor that smelled of coffee led to a one-bedroom studio flat that was considerably smaller than Rowan's old bedroom. A small kitchenette filled one side, with the bedroom and living room crammed into the remaining space, and a tiny bathroom was visible through a door on the right.

Despite its size, the flat already bore Rowan's signature touch. A stack of cages containing her tarantula collection occupied one corner, while the area in front of the bed was given over to her video game consoles underneath the TV mounted to the wall. Judging by the music emanating from that corner, my guess that she'd decided to spend her day off playing video games was on the mark. As far as I was concerned, the best part about her new abode was that not a single trace of her mother or sister remained.

Rowan beckoned me over to the kitchenette and began removing potion bottles from the cupboard. "There's got to be something in here that will help. Maybe try water first."

"Sure." I put Tansy in the sink and ran the tap over her feet. She yelped at the shock of the cold water, but it was better than her hanging limply in my hands. Some of the stickiness came loose from her feet, but it was hard to grab when she kept hopping around, tail flicking and splashing water over me.

Rowan held out a bottle and upended the contents on Tansy's feet, bringing her to a halt. "That ought to do it."

I grabbed my familiar's feet again and managed to unravel the sticky strand this time around, getting another soaking for my trouble.

"That smells vile," Tansy griped.

"It worked." Rowan gestured at Tansy's feet as she kicked the remnants of the sticky substance away from her. "Better?"

"Much better." Tansy jumped out of the sink, splattering the pair of us with water again.

I turned the tap off and grabbed a towel to dry myself.

After I passed the towel to Rowan, she gestured at the game consoles blinking invitingly against the back wall. "Want to play?"

"Sure." I joined her on the sofa, where her tarantula familiar, Ralph, sat entranced by the large TV screen. "Sorry to be the bearer of bad news, by the way, but it was Myrtle who led Tansy into the trap. I thought I saw a magpie outside the café, and Tansy offered to follow her."

Rowan groaned. "Not this again."

"I can talk to your mother and make it clear that sending her familiar to stalk you isn't cool."

She picked up the controller. "Why would she trap your familiar in a giant spiderweb though?"

"Tansy ran into it outside your back garden. I guess Aunt Shannon didn't want anyone else getting ideas about spying."

"Or me." She gave a short laugh. "I'm not exactly welcome there anymore."

I gave her a sympathetic nudge. "Nor me, but it's like being banned from the worst restaurant in town. Hardly worth shedding a tear over."

She laughed again, more genuinely this time. "You've got that right."

She loaded up the video game, and we put the subject of Aunt Shannon and her scheming familiar to the backs of our minds. For the moment, anyway.

7

The following morning, I looked upon a mountain of paperwork as if hoping it'd organise itself. Which it already had, kind of, because Chloe had already lovingly prepared it into stacks according to main topic, the way I'd requested during my first week on the job. There was just so *much* of it.

"You'd think there'd be a spell to digitise all this," I remarked.

Chloe glanced up from her own, much neater desk. "If someone's invented one, it hasn't caught on yet."

No surprises there. Why most of the coven members couldn't bring themselves to actually use the expensive computers they all had in their offices would forever remain a mystery to me. You'd think that practicality would win out over tradition at some point, given the lack of storage space. Considering they'd been using the same headquarters for a hundred years or more, it was a wonder the whole place hadn't collapsed under all the paperwork.

I moved the nonurgent papers to one side of the desk and handed off the correspondence to Chloe, who'd learned to mimic a neater version of my handwriting almost exactly. As long as I dictated to her what to write, I could get away with using her as a proxy rather than risking accidentally spelling the recipient's name wrong. As I'd learned the hard way already, even a spellchecker charm had its limits.

Grandma's ghost appeared at my shoulder. "What in the goddess's name is that?"

"What, exactly?" Being Grandma, she might be referring to anything from a slightly misaligned piece of paper to my Pikachu socks. "The sceptre? I told you, I can access it more easily if it's next to my desk. I'm pretty sure it doesn't have any strong opinions on being kept on the floor rather than in a glass case."

We'd had the same argument a dozen times already. If the sceptre had been the same size as a wand, then I could have fit it up my sleeve or in my pocket, but instead, I had to work with what I had.

Grandma tutted. "That wasn't it, but you really ought to have more respect for the sceptre. It's older than you are."

"So is the stack of receipts I found in the locked drawer of your desk. Did you keep *everything* from your time as Head Witch?"

"Yes."

Typical. The back of my office was tidier than it'd been when I'd first started working here, but that was because I'd had to block off the hole in the wall behind the endless cabinets that had enabled a rat shifter to sneak in and out of my office and attempt to bump me off. Yet I still hadn't begun to scratch the surface on dealing with the years of accumulated junk. It didn't help that Grandma had been more annoyed with my rearranging her office than with the fact that I'd taken her place as Head Witch.

"Not anymore." I indicated the overflowing wastepaper basket. "Anyway, what were you asking me about?"

"That." She indicated the background on my laptop, which depicted the various evolutions of Eevee. "Why did you put aliens on my laptop?"

"They're Pokémon. Also, you've never even used this laptop."

She gave me a wounded look as if I'd personally desecrated her grave. "The Head Witch is supposed to present herself in a professional manner. Putting poker-men on your screen is not appropriate."

I debated correcting her on the name but decided to let that one slide. "I'm sure the coven will survive. I happen to know at least one council member has a Lady Gaga video as her screensaver."

Grandma floated off, saying, "Not appropriate! Also, there's another pile of papers there. I think they're for you."

I groaned.

It was a relief when five thirty rolled around and it was time to leave the office for the evening. Tansy came scampering up to me on my way out of the building. She wasn't limping like she had been the day before, but she wasn't quite back to her bright-eyed and bushy-tailed self yet.

"Have fun today?" I asked her.

"More than you, I'll bet," she replied. "Do you really

want to sit and watch sports? I never thought you had the interest."

I shrugged. "I don't mind."

"Not when it's Harvey who's playing, I bet." She scampered ahead of me, towards the house. "At least there's plenty of trees to climb."

I reached the doorstep of the house. "Is Mum in there?"

"She's still in her office. I saw her on my way out."

"Good." I unlocked the door and headed straight upstairs to change into more suitable clothes for watching people play sports in a muddy field. I then grabbed my camera and the sceptre before leaving the house again.

Seeing Tansy watching Aunt Shannon's doorstep, I asked, "Is *she* around?"

"No," Tansy growled. "She was in her office too."

"I wonder what she's up to." I hadn't seen Aunt Shannon that day, so I had yet to confront her about the mysterious web Tansy had walked into near her house or her attempts to spy on her estranged daughter. "And that magpie?"

"Nowhere to be seen."

"Wonder if she's watching Rowan."

If Aunt Shannon didn't leave her youngest daughter alone, I might have to shelve my resolution to keep the peace for the time being. The two of us had barely spoken since her attempt to install Vanessa as the winner in the familiar contest had ended in disaster, and while she reluctantly came to meetings with the rest of the witch council, she stubbornly ignored me every time I spoke. Hardly the worst outcome, all things considered.

"When she isn't putting spiderwebs around her house," added Tansy. "Where'd she even get that thing from?"

"Haven't a clue." I veered onto the woodland trail, where Tansy leapt onto my shoulder instead of climbing trees as she usually would. "Don't worry. I doubt she'll have set up any traps in the forest."

"I don't trust her," she muttered into my ear.

"Neither do I, but she won't have put them anywhere that isn't her house. Not if she wanted to avoid being swarmed by the local wildlife."

Nevertheless, Tansy didn't budge from my shoulder as we walked down the woodland trail, heading towards the sports field at the western edge of town where the Sky Hopper team held their practise sessions.

"We can have a look around after practise if it's bugging you," I added. "If I speak to Aunt Shannon now, then I can guarantee the whole family will find out where we're going. It's bad enough that Ramsey knows."

"He didn't say no though." She hopped off my shoulder when we neared the practise field, while I walked more slowly than necessary in order to savour the fresh air after yet another day in the office. I might have got used to the routine, but that didn't mean I'd ever *like* being trapped indoors during my working hours after having experienced the alternative.

Several red-clad players had already gathered out on the field. When he saw me coming, Harvey walked over to greet me. "Glad you could make it."

"It's good to be outside after being in the office all day," I replied. "Where should I sit?"

"There is fine." He pointed to the benches at the end of the field. "Anyone can watch, technically, though we planned to keep the audience small for Gabriel's first session so he doesn't get too freaked out."

"I'll try not to distract him."

"One person isn't an issue," he told me. "It's when other teams try to sneakily watch our practise to get ideas that we have a problem."

"I bet." At least it wasn't raining. The team practised several times a week, no matter the weather—which, in England, was a risky prospect. "I hope it goes well."

"Thanks." He smiled at me, and that alone was worth the price of admission—namely, having to deal with grief from my family. If it ended in a proper date though, I'd happily sit through ten hours of sports, never mind a single practise session.

I took a seat on the bench and screwed around on my Pokémon Go account while waiting for the rest of the players to show up. Tansy amused herself by scaling the nearby trees and frightening the local birds until Harvey blew a whistle and sent a flock of startled pigeons scattering.

"Everyone over here," he called out.

The team assembled around him, clad in their bright-red uniforms, and lined up with the Falcons on one side and the Vultures on the other. I recognised Everly and Gwen among the latter—as well as Tomas. Now bandage free, he nevertheless wore a visibly disgruntled expression and stood apart from the rest of his team members.

Gabriel, meanwhile, stood slightly apart from the other Falcons, a head shorter than the other players and with his knees visibly trembling with nerves.

Harvey surveyed his players. "It's good to see you all. I've had a couple of people ask if it's right that we should be practising today, so soon after Jansen's untimely passing. I think he'd want us to be here though, and he'd certainly want us to be ready for our upcoming game. I think we should all keep him in mind when we practise and do our best for him. Deal?"

"Deal," everyone chorused.

"Good," said Harvey. "We'll start with some basic exercises, just to get our new player used to the routine. If all goes well, we'll progress to the more advanced techniques. Get your broomsticks ready."

They did so—Tomas with notable reluctance—and Harvey grabbed a basket of hoops. While the team members mounted their brooms, he shouted instructions at them, and they moved in synchrony, evidently having done this countless times before. As hoops flew back and forth and broomsticks wheeled in the air, I gave up trying to understand the rules and focused instead on how very attractive Harvey looked as he strode up and down the pitch, correcting his players' technique.

Everything seemed to be going well until a stray hoop hit Gabriel in the face. He dropped in the air, clinging to his broom one-handed and narrowly catching the hoop with his other hand.

"Who threw that?" Harvey called out.

"Tomas did," someone answered.

On his broom nearby, Tomas scowled. "It was an accident. I forgot how much smaller than Jansen he is."

"A likely story," Gwen said in a carrying whisper.

Tomas shot a glare towards her. "It's true."

"Enough," Harvey told them. "Resume practise, and don't let it happen again."

I kept an eye on Tomas as practise continued. He was

barely trying to catch any hoops that flew his way, though he didn't hesitate to criticise the others. When Gabriel missed a catch, Tomas shouted, "That was pathetic. A five-year-old could have done better."

"That's enough," Harvey told him. "Vultures, get into formation."

Crimson faced, Gabriel descended to pick up the hoop where it'd fallen onto the pitch. Tomas was too busy glowering at him to notice Gwen moving towards his position, and the two collided in a crash that knocked both of them off their brooms. Luckily, they weren't high enough off the ground to do more than wind themselves, but I still winced when they toppled into a tangle of limbs.

Gwen launched to her feet. "What is wrong with you?"

Tomas clambered upright, his nose bleeding. "It wasn't my fault."

"You weren't paying any attention," Everly called to him. "You were supposed to be in formation, not gawping at Gabriel."

As the rest of the team started shouting, too, Harvey called out, "Everyone land."

The team descended, while Tomas grabbed his broom and marched across the pitch, away from the others.

"I didn't say you could leave," Harvey told him.

"I've heard it all before," Tomas growled without turning around. "We shouldn't even be practising given that they haven't caught Jansen's killer yet."

A collective gasp rose among several of the other team members.

"I told you," Harvey said in calm tones, "Jansen would want us to continue to practise."

"Not with his killer among us," Tomas retaliated.

Several more gasps ensued.

Seemingly unimpressed, Gwen jabbed a finger at him. "You didn't care when he was alive. You're just trying to make excuses for your own shoddy technique."

"Nobody here was responsible for Jansen's death," Cole protested. "How can you say such a thing about your own teammates, Tomas?"

"Who did it then?" Tomas challenged. "We all know one another best, don't we?"

"That is enough." Harvey raised his voice. "It's clear to me that some of you aren't on your best form. I'd rather not have to impose consequences on any of you while you're grieving your teammate's death, so I'm going to give you all the time you need to calm down before our next session."

"He doesn't deserve that," Gwen muttered. "He accused us of murder."

"I'm captain," Harvey reminded them as several other team members professed their agreement. "Besides, we're all having a difficult time this week. We'll meet again on Wednesday, at the same time as usual. If anyone can't make the session or has an objection, you can let me know before then in private. *Not* while we're already at practise. Deal?"

"I've had enough." Tomas marched away, while I debated using the sceptre to fire a freezing spell at him from behind and pretend it was an accident. His behaviour towards his teammates was utterly uncalled for, and while he was the one who'd brought up Jansen's death, he'd acted more suspiciously than the rest of them put together.

At Harvey's command, the rest of the team began to

depart from the playing field. When Gwen and Everly came to the benches to pick up their bags, I heard the latter saying, "He's not even trying to hide the fact that he wants Gabriel off the team."

"Or to get kicked off himself," added Gwen. "Not that he doesn't deserve it."

"Is he always like this?" I asked them. "Because he's hardly demonstrating good sportsmanship."

"Not always," Everly commented. "It's only in the last week or two that he's been unbearable. Harvey ought to have put him on probation."

"I'm surprised Harvey *didn't* force him to straighten out his act or quit," I replied. "Did he start acting weird after Jansen announced his retirement?"

"Not until our last game," Gwen said. "Frankly, he was a mess at that game, which is why I didn't shed a tear when he got walloped off his broom after he let the other team bulldoze me."

"So, right after Jansen picked his replacement," I concluded.

"Yeah..." Everly hesitated. "But he *is* our teammate, and I don't think he's the one who killed Jansen, if that's what you were thinking. If you ask me, he feels guilty because he never apologised to him before his death, so he's taking it out on Gabriel."

"He didn't apologise to us either," said Gwen. "Harvey doesn't want us blaming one another though. Jansen wouldn't want that either."

"No, but we want the case solved, right?" I looked between them. "This is an outside perspective, mind you, but he seems to *hate* Gabriel. Do either of you have any idea why?"

"No clue," said Everly. "Ah… there's the captain."

Feeling a pang of guilt, I looked up to see Harvey approaching the stands. "Hey."

He ran a hand through his hair. "That… didn't quite go as planned."

"I'm sorry."

"It's not your fault." His gaze followed Gwen and Everly's departure. "I guess not everyone was ready for this practise session."

"Meaning Tomas. Want me to hit him with the sceptre?"

He managed half a smile. "Better not."

"I know there are mitigating circumstances, but he can't get away with accusing his teammates of murder," I protested. "You… you don't think he was trying to divert blame from himself, do you?"

His expression shadowed. "No, I don't think so. He might not be acting like himself lately, but everyone's shaken up by what happened."

"I don't want to overstep," I said carefully, "but the others said he was acting weirdly during the last game as well, right after Jansen announced his replacement. Gwen said that he completely failed to stop the enemy team from nearly knocking her out of the air."

He grimaced. "Tomas certainly wasn't on top form, it's true, but I wouldn't go as far as to make any connections with Jansen's death. I don't suppose your brother has an update on the investigation?"

"If he does, he didn't tell me." I couldn't shake the feeling that I'd let Harvey down by failing to convince my brother to let me help out. "I can drop by the police station and see if he's around."

He shook his head. "No, it's fine. I think we might have to reschedule our meal though. I think some of my team members are waiting to talk to me."

I looked past him, my face heating when I spotted Cole and some of the others waiting on the pitch. I hoped they hadn't heard my comments about Tomas, but I couldn't possibly be the only person who'd raised their eyebrows at his wild accusations during their practise session.

"That's no problem. I should go then."

As much as I wanted a proper date with Harvey, his team needed him as well. I wouldn't be selfish enough to take their captain away from them at a time like this.

"It won't always be like this," he added in a low voice. "Honestly."

"I know." I forced a smile. "Sorry if I made it worse."

"No, not at all. You made it a lot better, in fact."

That helped. "I'm glad to hear that."

While he turned his attention to the rest of the team, I went looking for Tansy. At least we'd have more time to check out the area behind Aunt Shannon's house to see how many traps she'd set up for unsuspecting familiars. Not that I'd rather do that than go on a date with Harvey, but it was better than facing my mother. No doubt Ramsey had told her all about my invitation to watch the practise session, and she'd be waiting to ambush me with questions.

As for Ramsey, he might not appreciate it, but I fully intended to let him know exactly what Tomas had done. The sooner we got to the bottom of his grudge against Gabriel, the better for everyone involved.

8

———

"No date then?" Tansy met me at the edge of the pitch. "What a letdown."

"Blame that Tomas for ruining the practise session. Did you see?"

"No, I was raiding the local grey squirrels' nut stores."

I snorted. "Well, Tomas was too busy bullying Gabriel to focus on the game. When the others called him out on it, he got all defensive and used Jansen's death to guilt them into stopping the session."

"And now everyone wants to complain at Harvey?"

"Nah, they don't blame him for it." They seemed to adore him, actually, which I could fully understand. "It's that Tomas who's got trouble written all over him. He was acting like a toddler jealous over someone else playing with his toys, and to top it off, he accused the rest of the team of murdering Jansen."

"Wow," said Tansy. "That's a guilty conscience talking if I ever saw one."

"Tell me about it."

Yet Harvey had thought him innocent. He probably didn't *want* to accept the idea of one of his teammates being guilty, but in any case, it wasn't him I needed to convince. That honour went to my brother... assuming he'd even listen to me.

Tansy and I took the same route along the woodland trail we'd come in through. The nearer we drew to the house, the twitchier my familiar grew, until she hopped onto my shoulder instead of leaping through the branches. I felt a rush of anger towards Aunt Shannon for hurting my familiar *and* dampening her confidence in the process.

"Show me where you found the trap," I told her when we neared the area where the path snaked behind our row of houses.

"There." She pointed her little paw in the direction of Aunt Shannon's garden, which stood next door to ours.

I came to a dead stop when I saw Ramsey waiting on the other side of the fence, at the very back of my mother's garden. "What *are* you doing?"

I was pretty sure he hadn't set foot in the garden since we were kids, and even back then, he'd avoided playing in mud and climbing trees like the rest of us.

Ramsey eyed me over the fence. "I could ask you the same question."

"I walk in the woods at least once per day. You only come out here when one of the shifters is drunkenly howling at the moon or someone buries a body."

He flushed just a little, and I noticed he was breathing harder than usual. He hadn't followed me all the way to the sports field, had he? No way. He might be persistent, but he wouldn't go *that* far to make a point.

"Exactly." Tansy jumped onto the fence next to him. "Where's Prickles? Did you leave him behind?"

"He's in the house," said Ramsey. "As a matter of fact, I was hoping I might run into you."

"Likewise." I walked to the gate, resolving to resume hunting for hidden traps in the woods when my brother stopped lurking around. "How's the investigation?"

As I neared my brother, he lowered his voice. "Don't get mad at me, but some new evidence came in. I don't know what to make of it just yet, but it doesn't paint your friend Harvey in a great light."

Harvey. My hands shook on the gate's latch. "What do you mean by that?"

He shook his head. "The details don't matter."

I fumbled the gate. "You can't just say that and expect me to forget all about it."

Another shake of his head. "We can talk inside. Anyone might be listening out here."

"Like Myrtle." I rotated on my heel to scan the trees for the magpie, but I saw no signs of her. "She's probably too busy spying on Rowan and reporting back to her mother. Seriously though, you have to tell me what you found out."

He stepped aside when I walked through the gate and closed it behind me. "I came into possession of Jansen's mobile phone, and I found some messages he exchanged with the current captain last week. With Harvey."

My heart sank. "Like what?"

He was silent for a long moment while I locked the gate and obligingly walked with him past Mum's rows of carefully cultivated flower beds and patches of herbs. "Harvey was in charge of the team's finances, it seems, and he and Jansen were arguing about him not sending out payments on time. In fact, Jansen's messages imply that he intended to leave town and take up playing for another team if Harvey didn't give him the money."

"What?" That couldn't be right. Hadn't Jansen already announced his retirement by then? There was no real age limit on playing Sky Hopper, but surely even the most avid player would eventually want to give up before they suffered a serious injury. "Why would he do that?"

"Because Harvey *didn't* pay him on time," Ramsey said. "If I was given to taking conjecture as fact, the messages heavily imply that Harvey was blackmailing him into staying with the team."

"Did any of the messages actually say that?" He had to be mistaken. Blackmail wasn't Harvey's style at all, and besides, he and the former captain had been friends as well as teammates. "You only read one side of the conversation, didn't you?"

"Yes, but I've seen compelling evidence that Jansen was in quite a bit of debt, and playing Sky Hopper was the way he made money," he said. "I found out from his ex-wife, who showed up in town unexpectedly, and so far, the evidence backs up her claims."

His ex-wife was in town? "Are you sure *she* wasn't trying to badmouth him?"

"By all accounts, it was an amicable split," he replied. "Though she did ask if she was mentioned in his will."

"That was nice of her."

If she hadn't been around last Friday, then she couldn't have been directly responsible for his death, but her appearance struck me as suspicious to say the least.

"Have you questioned her then?"

"Not properly," he said. "She called the police and asked for the facts on his death, and she wanted to know who'd handle the debts afterwards. I looked into the matter and found that Jansen did owe some large sums of money for gambling and similar activities."

"And Harvey knew?"

Had the rest of the team too? It might explain Tomas's sudden attitude change if he hadn't previously been aware of the problem... but that didn't explain why anyone would suddenly want the former captain dead. His debts didn't impact the rest of the team, right?

"It seems he did," he said. "Harvey's the captain, so it's to be expected that the former captain would have given him that information. However, these messages... it sounds as though it was a point of contention between them."

"That doesn't imply Harvey's involvement in his death. People argue all the time. You should have seen the others at today's practise session." A moment passed. "*Did* you see them?"

"No, I didn't." His face reddened a little. "If you must know, I went to look for you in the forest in case you and Tansy ran into trouble. I'm glad to see that you didn't go off alone with the captain."

"He is *not* going to murder me, Ramsey. He didn't kill Jansen either."

"Might you be a little biased?"

Heat crept up my neck. "You're the one who's not supposed to let biases get in the way of his judgement. The messages you found are one-sided, and for all we know, Jansen did most of his communication with the rest of his team face-to-face."

"Nevertheless, I still have to look into the possible connection between the content of the messages and Jansen's death."

I scowled. Perhaps Harvey and Jansen had argued occasionally, but not everyone got along perfectly at all times. Case in point: me and my ever-stubborn brother. "Harvey can't have blackmailed him. It's not like him at all."

"You said yourself that the players take the game seriously," he said. "He's the captain, so I imagine that entails a great deal of responsibility as well as making hard decisions."

"That is *not* what I meant." I folded my arms across my chest. "You can't seriously think that someone who Jansen mentored personally would have killed him in cold blood. And don't give me that nonsense about the killer usually being close to the victim. I know how much Harvey respected and cared about Jansen. You only have to talk to him for five minutes to figure that out."

"You know him, do you?" he challenged. "Do you think your little crush is more worthy than the experience of my team?"

Little crush? My face heated, and the chirp of birdsong from the nearby bird feeders took on a threatening note. "I'd do the same for a friend, but I guess you wouldn't know about those either, would you?"

Tansy jumped onto my shoulder, her tail tickling my neck. Breathing hard, I looked past my brother to see none other than Harvey standing behind the house. My face went, if possible, even redder. How could I have failed to notice him there? What was he even doing in my mother's garden, for that matter?"

As if in response to my unasked question, he held up my camera, an apologetic look on his face. "You left this behind."

So I had. I took it from him, my neck burning. "Thanks."

"Who let you in?" Ramsey demanded.

Harvey blinked in surprise. "Your mother did."

"Ramsey," I hissed. "That's enough. Don't be rude."

"You're lucky I'm not currently on duty." Ignoring me, he advanced on Harvey. "You certainly shouldn't be in our house."

"Ramsey." I stepped firmly in front of my brother. "Ignore every word he says, Harvey."

"I can leave," Harvey said. "It isn't a problem. I only wanted to give your sister the camera back."

From his evident surprise, he didn't have the slightest idea that my brother might be planning to arrest him. He hadn't heard that part of our conversation… but he'd heard the ending.

"Go on," Ramsey ordered. "Get out of the house, and don't come back."

"Keep your hair on." I stuck close behind Harvey in case Ramsey tried hexing him when his back was turned, though I hadn't seen him use a hostile spell on anyone in years. "Sorry about him, Harvey."

Should I tell him about his impending arrest? Or might I be able to talk some sense into my brother before things escalated even further? I had to at least try, for Harvey's sake, but Ramsey was in one of his uncompromising moods, and I'd already thrown fuel onto the flames by insulting him.

"I get it," said Harvey. "He's probably stressed out

about the murder. Speaking of which, I need to go and reassure my teammates."

"Ignore what he said about not coming back." I spoke in a low voice as we made our way through the house. "He tends to overreact when he's under pressure. It'll be fine."

I feared I might have to eat those words later, but after the disastrous practise session, worrying about an impending arrest was the last thing Harvey needed. With Ramsey at home for the time being, I had to seize my chance to convince him to change his mind.

"I'll see you later." He left the house through the front door.

I waved goodbye and waited to be certain he was out of hearing distance before marching back to confront my brother behind the house. "What the hell was that? You're supposed to treat everyone as innocent until proven guilty, aren't you? Whatever so-called evidence you found doesn't warrant you acting like he's already bound for prison."

"That doesn't mean he has the right to walk into our house."

My gaze slid to the closed door to the living room. "I might add that our mother was the one who let him in, so you can take it up with her, not me."

"She doesn't know about the murder investigation," he said. "Not the latest, anyway, but after that, I'll be sure to set her straight on your friend's status on the suspect list."

All right. Disliking Harvey was one thing, but labelling him the number-one suspect in a murder based on said dislike was a step too far. He ought to know that. "Maybe wait for your temper to cool down before you arrest anyone."

My own anger had fuelled the birds into a frenzy, but Ramsey's control over his magic was as tight as the stick permanently wedged up his rear end.

I glared at him as he walked away while Tansy ran over from chasing pigeons with her tail in the air. "I'm guessing you don't want to go looking for traps then?"

"Not while there's a rabid Ramsey in the garden," I answered in an undertone. "Besides, I need to talk to Mum before he tells her Harvey is guilty."

Tansy huffed and ran to the bird feeder instead. I, meanwhile, entered the house again and went looking for my mother. As expected, I found her in the living room with a pile of paperwork and two sleeping cats.

"Who exactly was that man?" she asked without looking up.

"Harvey," I told her. "From the Sky Hopper team. He came to give me my camera back."

She lifted her head. "Where exactly did you leave it? I wasn't aware you saw him today."

Maybe I should have avoided this conversation altogether. "I went to watch the Sky Hopper team's practise session."

A twitch in her jaw. "Please tell me you at least took the sceptre with you."

"What do you take me for?" I held up the sceptre. "I didn't need to use it."

Not even to hit Tomas *or* to give Ramsey a thwack on the head, though both of them kind of deserved it.

"I won't repeat my warnings, Robin. You shouldn't be wandering around alone."

"I was with a man *you* let into the house," I pointed out. "And who Ramsey wants to arrest for a murder he never committed just to stop him from spending time with me."

"Ramsey did *what?*"

"He's lost his mind." Admittedly, I hadn't helped the situation, but he had zero reason to treat Harvey the way he had. "He chased Harvey out of the garden because he's convinced himself that spending time with me makes him guilty by default."

"That isn't true." Ramsey himself appeared in the doorway. "He's a suspect I'm watching because of some messages he exchanged with the victim. I was concerned for Robin's safety."

At that, I did reach out and poke him in the arm with the sceptre. "Robin can speak for herself. And Ramsey needs to chill out."

Mum rose to her feet. "Don't worry, Ramsey. I won't let him into the house again."

"I thought you taught him better manners," I said pointedly. "If Harvey turns out to be innocent, he's within his rights to tell everyone the Wildwood Coven is rude and unwelcoming to guests."

"He's no guest." He turned away. "I'm going back to the office."

"Dinner is in the oven," Mum said to his retreating back, but he didn't respond.

I heard the door close behind him, and my hands curled into fists. "He thinks Harvey killed his own team-mate, his friend, because of some dubious messages he read on Jansen's phone. He hasn't even seen the other side of their conversation. And *I* saw someone at their practise session who was practically announcing his guilt for the world to see."

"I wouldn't know." Mum sat down again. "I rather

think Ramsey has more sense than to arrest an innocent man though."

"He's not acting rationally," I pressed. "He's decided he hates Harvey because of me electing to spend time with him instead of fulfilling my duties as Head Witch."

"I really don't know what you expect me to do about it, Robin."

My shoulders slumped. "He won't listen to me, but he'd listen to you if you told him to tone it down. You know that."

"I can't stop him from doing his job."

That wasn't remotely what I was asking, but I knew when I was beaten. Retreating to my room, I put my camera down on my bedside table. I hadn't even remembered to take any pictures of the practise session...

Wait a moment. I'd completely forgotten my attempts to snap pictures of the Sky Hopper team at the party... which meant I had actual photographic evidence of the moments leading up to Jansen's death.

Might there be a clue in there that would help Harvey prove his innocence where my words alone had failed?

I sat down on my bed and turned on the camera, loading up the pictures I'd taken at the party. Most were pretty similar, depicting the crowded table I'd sat at and the people jostling to get into the frame. Each picture of the team contained a crush of background figures and elbows and knees in the way of the view, and my optimism began to flag when I reached the end with no new clues to speak of.

I started from the beginning of the photos again, moving more slowly this time. The first shot showed Harvey sitting close to me, his captain's badge gleaming on his coat. The background was less crowded in that picture, so I zoomed in on the image a little. All the team members were at the table except Tomas. He sat alone at the bar, as I remembered...but when I zoomed in, something gleamed next to him on the bar.

A badge? If he'd had the badge that Jansen had choked on right next to him, then this might be all the evidence I needed to prove Tomas's guilt before Harvey was arrested for murder.

9

I was ready to pounce on my brother and show him the photos the instant he entered the house, but he didn't come back that night, and Mum refused to let me message him and drag him home from the office. So I gave up and went to bed, though sleep was elusive. I knew I should be resting for my next long day as Head Witch, but it was hard to forget that Harvey's freedom might depend on my ability to convince my brother he wasn't a murderer.

The following morning, I tried not to doze off at my desk while I looked over the day's schedule. Among other things, I had a long meeting with the council, which included Aunt Shannon. While I felt bad for giving up on my attempt to help Tansy search for evidence of her nasty spider traps in the forest, picking a fight with my aunt while my brother and I were still at loggerheads would not have been the wisest idea. We'd retained a chilly silence during previous meetings, but that would change when I inevitably brought up her latest antics.

Grandma's ghost appeared behind me. "You're back. Have you been practising using that sceptre?"

Not unless you count poking my brother. Maybe I should have given it a test run on Tomas after all.

"I have a three-hour meeting to get to, so our next magic lesson will have to wait until later," I informed her. "I don't suppose you can let me hang out on the other side of the grave for a few hours instead?"

"Not unless you want to stay here." She gave a laugh that sounded more like a cackle. "I wouldn't object to the company, if that's what you want."

I suppressed a shudder. "No, thanks."

Leaving my desk behind, I made my way to the large room in which the council typically held their meetings. I'd grown used to the way everyone's eyes watched me enter the room and take up my position at the centre of the table, and the derision in Aunt Shannon's expression when she took a seat at the opposite end of the table barely registered. Mum sat on my right, and the others filed into the room around me in a rustle of cloaks.

When everyone was seated, I called the meeting to a start. One of the coven's many ridiculous traditions dictated that I had to make the same speech regardless of what the meeting was actually about, but it was hardly one of the more heinous tasks appointed to the Head Witch.

"On the agenda for the day…" I consulted the paper I'd brought from my desk and read the items on the list one at a time, my heart giving an unpleasant lurch when I reached the last one. "…and the matter of meeting the other Head Witches."

"We'll start with that," Aunt Shannon ventured. "I'm

sure I'm not the only person wondering when the Head Witch is going to meet her equals."

Mockery dripped from her words, while my hands fisted under the table. My aunt hadn't said a word to me during our last five meetings, but as soon as the chance to humiliate me arose, she leapt on it. Never mind that it wasn't up to me to decide when the other Head Witches would have time to come to Wildwood Heath.

"That depends on the other Head Witches' schedules."

"Exactly," Mum put in. "I've already told you that we need every Head Witch to be in agreement as to the date and time of the meeting. There's also the matter of the location. Unless you want to put Wildwood Heath down as your nomination, we need to wait for the other Head Witches to offer their own suggestions before making a decision."

When the inevitable day arrived for me to meet the other Head Witches, I wouldn't necessarily object to it taking place in a familiar setting, but the one perk of my new job was being occasionally allowed to travel outside of the town to meet other Head Witches. This meeting would be the first and only chance I'd have to leave Wildwood Heath in a while… but being on unfamiliar territory would put me at even more of a disadvantage compared to the other, more experienced witches.

"*Does* anyone want to nominate the town?" I addressed the council as a whole. "I'd be willing to do so if we all agree."

Mum glanced sideways at me. "As would I."

I was pretty sure that was the first time she'd agreed with me without hesitation, but in meetings, her main priority was not letting anyone undercut the Head Witch —and by "anyone," I meant Aunt Shannon.

The others murmured agreement, to my surprise, while Aunt Shannon's lips pursed. "I will support the idea as well. I think Wildwood Heath has a lot to offer."

Too late, it hit me that staying in town would enable my aunt to twist the situation to her advantage, but I'd already put the idea forwards, and the benefits would still outweigh the downsides.

"That's settled then," I told the council as a whole. "What next?"

The discussion returned to other, safer topics, but Aunt Shannon kept giving me the occasional glance when she thought I wasn't looking, a scheming glint in her eye that I didn't like in the slightest. If anyone intended to sabotage the impression I made on the other Head Witches, it was my aunt. I'd need to watch my step.

I hadn't figured out how to bring up the subject of Rowan, either, to say nothing of Aunt Shannon's possible involvement in my familiar's injury the other day. Familiars were allowed into the meeting room, but Tansy generally spent her time outside in the back garden, unwilling to sit still for an extended period of time. Since Myrtle wasn't around either, I hoped she wasn't causing trouble for my familiar *or* spying on Rowan. It grew progressively more difficult to keep my focus on the subject of the meeting, but since half the items on the list concerned petty disputes about flower arrangements in the coven's garden, I figured it was a small miracle that I didn't fall asleep instead of pretending to listen. Pity I had yet to learn how to use the sceptre to conjure up a Robin-shaped statue that could sit in meetings in my place, because for now, my only option was to let them argue it out until they ran out of steam.

When the meeting dragged to a halt, I gave my obligatory closing speech and left the room before anyone could mention begonias again. Since it was my lunch break, I sought out Tansy in the garden and then went out the front door.

Mum cleared her throat from behind me. "Robin, where are you going?"

I spoke over my shoulder without pausing. "The café."

"You know we have a perfectly good chef at home, don't you?"

"Yes, but I wanted to see if Rowan was around." Not a lie, because I did need to update her on her mother's shenanigans. "I'll be back within the hour. Don't worry."

After I reached the high street, I made straight for the police station. Tansy scurried alongside me, tail flashing bright red, while I speed-walked through the automatic doors to the station.

Ramsey wasn't in the lobby, so I walked to his office and knocked on the door.

"Excuse me?" the receptionist called from behind me. "You can't just walk in here… oh, it's you, Head Witch."

Ramsey answered the door with a long-suffering look on his face. "Not again, Robin."

"I thought you'd like to know that I have evidence for you."

"Evidence of what?"

I pulled my camera out of my bag. "It slipped my mind that I snapped a few photos at the party right before Jansen died, but I thought there might be something of interest in there."

When he didn't budge, I thrust the camera under his nose and showed him the zoomed-in part of the photo which displayed Tomas's position at the bar.

"What am I supposed to be looking at?"

"Doesn't that thing on the table look like a badge to you?" I indicated the spot in front of Tomas with my fingernail. "Tomas spent the party sulking after he got so riled up during the game that he let himself get knocked off his broom. According to the other players, his bad mood started at precisely the moment Jansen announced that Gabriel would be taking his place."

"That's not a badge, Robin," he said. "It's a coaster."

"How do you know that?" I peered at the photo, but the angle did make it hard to be a hundred percent certain. "Looks like a badge to me."

"This is flimsy evidence, Robin. How would the badge have made it all the way into the victim's cake slice from over there?"

"Magic?" I suggested. "Everyone on that team has ample experience using their wands to levitate hoops around. Moving a badge would be easy by comparison. It's hardly less substantial evidence than half a text-message argument."

"This doesn't prove your friend's innocence, Robin."

"I never said it did. Have you questioned him again? Or checked *his* phone?"

"Our next interview is scheduled for this afternoon," he said. "And no, you can't watch."

"I only came here to give you this." I waved the camera at him. "Are you just going to ignore the actual footage of the party I captured?"

"I'll look at the photos later." He indicated the desk. "Leave the camera here."

I put down the camera on the desk, next to Prickles. "You should talk to Tomas again. He's hiding something, whether it's related to the murder or not. He wouldn't treat his teammates so badly for no reason."

"I'm still working through the list of people who were at the party," he said tiredly. "Unless more evidence comes along, as was the case with the victim's phone, I can't afford to spend time questioning people I've already spoken to."

"Except Harvey."

"You aren't going to let this drop, are you?"

"No, because I know he didn't do it."

"That's for the proof to decide, Robin."

I hadn't given up on getting hold of proof yet, but I'd have to get a touch more creative if the photos alone weren't enough to convince Ramsey of Harvey's innocence.

As I left the police station, I spotted Gabriel walking out of a nearby shop. Figuring I couldn't get myself into any more trouble than I already had, I went to talk to him. "Hey."

Gabriel jumped. "Oh. Hi, Head Witch."

"I told you that you didn't have to call me that, didn't I?"

I watched Tansy scale a drainpipe nearby, in pursuit of a nearby crow.

"I was watching the practise session yesterday evening. Tomas was way out of line in how he treated you."

He flushed. "I understand why. It was too soon after Jansen's death for us to start practising again."

"That's no excuse for how he acted towards you though," I insisted. "Did the two of you know one another before you joined the team?"

"No." He didn't quite meet my eyes though, and suspicion kindled in my chest.

"I'm not reporting to my brother." I dropped my voice. "I'd rather he doesn't know I'm talking to you, in fact."

He blinked. "Why?"

I surreptitiously looked around in case anyone was listening in. "The truth is, it's starting to look like Harvey will be the one to take the blame, so anything you can tell me which might help me prove he isn't responsible for Jansen's death would be more than welcome."

The colour drained from his face. "Not Harvey. The police can't think *he* did it, can they?"

"That's why I'm trying to find out anything that might help to prove he didn't."

His shoulders slumped. "I… all right. I'll talk to you."

"Let's go in there." I indicated Were's My Coffee? "I was planning to grab lunch anyway, since I have to be back in the office in forty minutes. Let's make this quick."

Rowan was working the lunchtime shift, and she arched a brow when she saw me walk into the café with Gabriel. The flow of customers meant we didn't have any time to chat, so I bought a sandwich and took it to the only free table.

Upon joining me, Gabriel said, "I really don't know much, Head Witch. I'm not sure I can be of any help."

"Let's start with Tomas then," I decided. "Did he and Jansen get along at all?"

"They used to." He shook his head. "So the others say, anyway. I didn't know him back then."

"Why would he object to you joining the team?"

He shrugged one shoulder. "He's been in a mood all week, and it's worse now. He was in the middle of an argument with Jansen when he died, and now he knows he'll never get closure."

"But does he have anything against you in particular?" I pressed. "Did he think someone else might take the position, or would he have behaved the same if someone else had got the title as well?"

He glanced over his shoulder. "I don't know. We've never spoken until now."

Was he telling the truth? Tomas looked far guiltier of the pair of them, but his sudden and irrational animosity didn't strike me as the sort one would throw at a stranger.

I thought back to the photograph and the clear shape of the badge sitting on the bar next to him. "If you thought of someone who might think it was funny to force the former captain to choke on his own badge, is he the person who'd first come to mind?"

Gabriel flinched. "I can't... I can't say for sure. I mean, he's been on the team longer than I have, and he could easily turn the evidence against me."

"Do you think he'd do that?" Whatever his reasons, would he try to direct blame at Gabriel instead? Or was it Harvey he wanted to frame? *Those messages...*

When he didn't respond, I said, "I heard that Harvey and Jansen had a pretty rough argument not long before his death. Did they seem to be getting along when they gave you the position?"

He blinked. "Is that why the police think Harvey killed him?"

"They don't, but I'd like to hear your perspective. Did you hear or see them talking to one another at all?"

"They seemed fine with one another at my trial, but I didn't see them again until the party. Maybe it was different at their match. I don't know. Why did they argue?"

"Something about money," I hedged. "Is Harvey the one who handles the team's finances?"

"I think he is, but I don't know the details. I haven't been paid yet."

That made sense. The other team members were more likely to be able to give me the relevant information, but I didn't want to let them all know Harvey's precarious status, especially Tomas.

"Do you know anything about Jansen's family?" I asked instead.

He shook his head. "No. Someone said he was married once…"

"Apparently his ex-wife is in town." Come to think of it, she hadn't visited the police yet, unless I counted her phone call the previous day. She might be worth talking to. "Anyway, thanks for the help."

"I wasn't much help, was I?" His face fell. "I don't want Harvey to be arrested. I wish I'd paid more attention at the party, but there were people everywhere, and I was overwhelmed."

"I know." I picked up my half-eaten sandwich and dropped the remains into the bin. "Thanks anyway."

I waved at Rowan on my way out, since she was still busy dealing with an endless flow of customers, and then nearly tripped over Tansy outside the door. "Whoa. What's up?"

"That magpie!" she exclaimed. "She took off again before I could catch her."

"Rowan's tied up, or I'd tell her." That would have to wait until later though. "C'mon, let's head back to the office. Maybe she's there."

"Not likely." Tansy cast a disgruntled look at the café before sweeping away down the high street. "How'd your chat with Gabriel go?"

I gave a shrug. "He didn't know much, but he's new to the team. I did remember Jansen's ex-wife is staying in town, so I'll have to talk to her later as well."

"Good idea." She bounded ahead of me. "I can poke around the inns to see which one she is staying at if you like."

"Are you sure?"

"Of course I am. No magpies will be hovering around *there*."

She was probably right, but I renewed my mental reminder to help her look for proof against Aunt Shannon as soon as possible. "All right. Come and let me know if you see Myrtle anywhere she shouldn't be, okay?"

After parting ways with my familiar, I headed back to the office and another afternoon of joyless admin. Better than a meeting with Aunt Shannon, but not much.

Ramsey wouldn't be pleased with me for going behind his back, but since he hadn't noticed me talking to Gabriel this time around, I could only conclude that he was too busy interviewing Harvey to bother with anything I had to say.

Was Harvey going through interrogation right now? Had I made things worse by talking to Ramsey myself? Questions circled my mind like low-flying birds and made it even more difficult than usual to focus on my next lesson with Grandma. By that point, I was starting to think that using the sceptre to bash assailants on the head was a more viable plan after all.

After I turned everything in the office purple, including Chloe and Carmilla, Grandma declared me a hopeless case. "You ruined my cabinets!"

"You're the one who decided we had to practise in your office," I pointed out. "Really, this is about the worst place possible for practising using a volatile magical instrument. It's like testing a live bomb in a closet."

"Then by all means, go outside if you want to humiliate yourself."

I wasn't opposed to the idea of getting out of the stuffy room, but the idea of another magical mishap in front of anyone from the Henbane Coven who happened to be peering over the fence did not appeal. "An empty classroom would be better. Somewhere there isn't years' worth of paperwork or poor Chloe trying to do her work without being turned purple."

"Always with the excuses." Grandma's ghost vanished in a flash. I wondered if she *had* gone to find a classroom, but she didn't return.

Chloe gave me a sympathetic look. "I don't mind being used as a guinea pig, for the record."

"Sorry I turned you purple." I lowered the sceptre. "It seems a waste of time to practise every single spell I could just use a wand for, with a fraction of the effort and less chance of anyone being turned the colour of a plum."

"If it helps, your grandmother rarely used it."

Carmilla snorted. "Only because she wasn't in the

habit of walking headfirst into assassins the way you do, Robin."

"I don't recall ever walking headfirst into one."

Carmilla yawned. "So pedantic."

"You're one to talk." I returned to my desk. "Frankly, I'd take a swarm of assassins over another meeting about flower beds."

"Be careful what you wish for," said Carmilla.

10

After work finished for the day, I once again headed for the police station. I knew exactly what Ramsey would have to say about me showing my face at his office twice in a day, but I didn't really give a crap, to be honest. I needed to ensure Harvey wasn't behind bars—and I also wanted to know if Ramsey had had the chance to look at my photos from the party. I had an inkling I'd need to remind him, or else he'd forget altogether, which said volumes for how highly he valued my input.

"He didn't even want to know," I grouched at Tansy as we walked down the high street. "Honestly. For all his griping about needing evidence to prove anything, he didn't seem impressed with actual footage of the event."

"Maybe he thought you edited the photos with magic."

"He'd better not." I scowled. "If I was going to put a spell on the photos to pin the blame on someone who isn't Harvey, I'd have picked a less ambiguous way to go about it. Maybe by magically photoshopping Vanessa into it or something."

Tansy snorted. "Speaking of certain relatives of yours…"

"I'll come and help you look for traps later," I said. "Sorry. I keep getting diverted."

"You want to stop your boyfriend getting arrested. I get it."

"At this rate, he won't even have time to achieve boyfriend status before he's behind bars." I exhaled in a sigh. "Even if he hasn't actually been arrested yet, he's stuck with the guilty label on his head unless new evidence shows up."

"The good news," said Tansy, "is that I found out which inn Jansen's ex-wife is staying at. The Owl's Nest. She rented a private room."

I pressed my hand to my forehead. "I forgot. Thanks, Tansy."

"I do my best." She hopped onto my shoulder. "I nosed around her room, but she's not that interesting. She just brought a suitcase of essentials and that's it."

"Probably a good idea if she didn't expect to stay." Her behaviour didn't suggest she expected to be questioned by the police either, but she'd seemed more fixated on not being saddled with her ex-husband's debt than on the fact that someone had murdered him. "I'll find out how Harvey's interview went first."

My heart began beating faster, and I quickened my pace. I entered the police station as my brother was exiting his own office. When he caught sight of me, his jaw twitched. "What is it? If you want your camera back, I haven't had the chance to look through the photos yet. I've been doing interviews for the past few hours."

My heart lurched. "Have you made any arrests?"

"No."

I breathed more easily. "So Harvey didn't have any evidence against him."

"That's not what I meant." He strode over to me. "It takes time to come to a decision, and Harvey didn't deny sending those messages to Jansen."

That's not good. A conversation could be taken out of context, and one argument didn't mean Harvey was guilty of anything… but if word got out, then Harvey's reputation would take a hit, and the team itself might be tainted by association.

"Then I'd wait until you read the other side of the conversation before passing judgement," I said. "Also, if you're wondering if I used magic to mess with the photos from the party, I didn't. I forgot I even took them, in fact, but if you want to dismiss them as evidence, then I'd like to have my camera back."

"What?" he said blankly. "I didn't say anything about altering your photos using magic. Can you even do that?"

An unexpected surge of annoyance hit me. He wasn't ignoring my photos due to a belief that I'd altered them in an attempt to get Harvey off the hook after all, but I had to admit I was kind of insulted that he'd forgotten one of the few branches of magic I was more than passably decent at. One of the reasons I'd wanted the camera in the first place was to test my skill at magical photomanipulation.

"I'm out of practise, but yes." I backed towards the door. "See you later."

Once the automatic doors slid closed, Tansy looked up at me. "I don't think he meant to offend you."

"That's worse, if anything." I swatted away a pigeon that had flown over to me, drawn to the magic radiating outwards from my frustration. "I forgot to ask if he'd interviewed Jansen's ex-wife yet."

"I'm guessing not," Tansy replied. "Want me to see if she's in her hotel room?"

I debated for a moment. How far was I willing to go to prove Harvey's innocence? I'd already crossed lines with Ramsey, but he seemed determined to see a handful of messages as a reason to condemn Harvey while simultaneously dismissing the notion that the proof of Tomas's possession of the badge Jansen had choked on might be right there in the photographic evidence of the party.

"All right then, but make sure she doesn't see you."

Tansy scampered away while I made my casual way towards the redbrick building that housed the town's nicest inn, trying to look unobtrusive. A somewhat-tricky task with the sceptre in my hand, but I kept it half hidden behind my back until the flash of a red tail scaling down a drainpipe signalled Tansy's return.

"She's alone in her room. Want to go and talk to her?"

"Might as well." I strode into the Owl's Nest, where the blond shifter receptionist predictably jumped to attention when he saw the sceptre in my hand.

"Head Witch." He bowed his head. "How can I help you?"

"I'd like to talk to one of your guests," I said with all the authority I could muster.

"Of course," said the receptionist. "Which guest would that be?"

"Susie Christopher," Tansy whispered in my ear.

"Susie Christopher," I repeated. "I understand she's staying in a private room."

"Does she know you're here?" His gaze darted around the reception area. "It's not customary to allow members of the public to pay unexpected visits to our guests, but I'd gladly make an exception for you, Head Witch."

"We can talk elsewhere. I'd just like to let her know I'm here."

As much as I needed answers, I didn't want to abuse my position as Head Witch. I would have preferred not to play that card at all, in fact, but with Harvey on the brink of arrest, I needed to know where Jansen's ex-wife stood on the subject of his murder.

The receptionist briefly picked up the phone and spoke a few words into it before hanging up. "She's coming downstairs. Is that all right?"

"Sure." I waited, Tansy sitting on my shoulder, until footsteps came from the stairs.

A witch of average height and build descended into the lobby. She looked a little younger than Jansen had, though her blond hair had clearly been dyed recently, and she was heavily made up. A number of beaded necklaces hung around her neck and jangled with every step.

"Excuse me?" Her gaze went from the sceptre in my hand to my face. "Are *you* the Head Witch?"

"Yes, I am." What was with that tone? "If you don't mind, I have a couple of questions to ask about your ex-husband. Would you rather talk in your room or in here?"

I indicated the seats in the corner of the reception area, and the guy at the desk looked up. "Ah, I can leave and give you some privacy if you like. Anything you need, Head Witch."

Why not. "Thanks. We won't be long."

"I should hope *not*." Susie put her hands on her hips. "I have nothing to do with the Wildwood Coven whatsoever. I thought their leader was much older than you are, come to that."

"That was my grandmother," I explained. "So you used to live in Wildwood Heath?"

"Obviously I did," she said. "A little slow for a Head Witch, aren't you?"

I bit back a sarcastic comment. "I've been away from town until recently. Besides, this isn't coven business. It's to do with your ex-husband's murder."

"Murder." Susie sucked in a breath. "So it's true."

I frowned. "Didn't anyone tell you he was murdered?"

"They said he choked to death." She sniffed, her eyes beginning to water. "The police implied his death wasn't accidental when I called them to ask what had happened, but they haven't contacted me since."

"They will." I beckoned her to follow me to the seating area. "I can tell you the rest if you answer my questions. Is that okay?"

"Fine." She strode imperiously over to the corner and took a seat, her beads jangling. "How did my ex-husband die?"

"He choked to death on a badge that someone put into his slice of cake at his retirement party."

"Retirement?" She blew her nose into a handkerchief. "He finally gave up crashing into trees on a weekly basis?"

"He planned to retire, but someone killed him first."

Susie sniffed. "He didn't deserve that," she said hoarsely. "Not at all."

Hmm. According to what I'd heard so far, they hadn't split in an amicable manner, but that evidently didn't extend to her being glad of his fate. If she was being truthful, that was.

"I didn't think so either," I replied. "I was at the party myself, and nobody saw who was responsible for putting the badge into his cake slice."

"So the police have themselves in a bind, do they?"

Her tone implied she was fishing for gossip, which played into my plan nicely. "The police ruled it a homicide, but that's as far as they've got so far. When did you and your husband split up, anyway?"

"Two years ago," she replied. "Should have happened sooner, really, since I'd wanted to get out of this town for years. So did he, at first, but there were always excuses. Every single time we almost made plans to leave, something came up, generally involving that Sky Hopper team of his."

"He was captain until last year, so I imagine he didn't want to leave his team," I remarked. "Did you ever go to any of their matches?"

"A few. I wasn't really interested in sports." She stared into the distance for a moment. "Certainly not to the extent that he was, anyway."

Not necessarily a sign of her involvement in his death, though perhaps it explained one of the reasons they hadn't been a good fit. But what I really wanted to know was why she'd decided to come here so soon after his murder, before the police had contacted her.

"If you don't mind my asking, why did you come back to town?"

"I wanted to find out how Jansen died and to pay my respects," she said. "Isn't that enough?"

"That's fair," I acknowledged. She *had* lived here for years, after all. "I hope this isn't too intrusive to ask, but do you think he's likely to leave you anything in his will?"

"I doubt it," she said. "The house, maybe, but it probably needs to be sold to pay off all his debts."

Debts. Not the first time that word had come up, and his discussion on the subject with Harvey had led my brother to believe that blackmail had been involved in handling payments for his position on the team. If anyone knew the issue intimately, it was his ex-wife.

"Which debts would those be?" I asked. "I mean, did he gamble, or…?"

"Gambling, overspending… he was always hopeless with money," she said. "I imagine it got worse after our split, because I was no longer around to keep him from wasting every penny. I know for a fact that back when he was captain, he always had someone else take care of the team's finances."

Hang on. If Harvey was in charge of the team's finances now, then that hadn't necessarily been the case before he was captain. Even if he had been, then what Ramsey had taken for the threat of blackmail might have simply been the exasperation of someone who'd had to deal with the same arguments from an irresponsible spender a thousand times before.

"Was he always that bad?" I asked.

"Oh, yes," Susie said. "Drove me batty. Thank the

goddess we had separate bank accounts, or else he'd have pulled me straight down with him."

Hmm. "Do you know who on the team was in charge of handling the finances?"

"No," she said. "Like I said, I wasn't close to the rest of the team. It might have been anyone."

"If the police ask you about it, can you make it clear that Jansen had issues with handling money?" I asked. "Right now, they're accusing someone I believe to be innocent based upon an argument he and Jansen had about the team's finances, taken out of context."

"Really?" Her eyes rounded. "What argument?"

"Some messages on Jansen's phone implied that the current captain was withholding money from him," I explained. "This was shortly before his death, so the police thought the timing was suspicious, but I imagine the captain was well aware of his problems with money."

"I have no doubt that's true." She sighed. "I hoped he'd change his ways, you know."

Another thought occurred to me. "The messages implied that Jansen threatened to leave town and join another team if they didn't pay him. Does that sound familiar?"

A groan escaped her. "Yes, it does."

That settled it then. "If it's okay with you, I'd like to tell the chief of police what you just told me. It might just spare an innocent man from a jail sentence."

"Oh, absolutely." She sat up straighter. "I want the right person brought to justice."

"Same here," I said. "Is there anything else you'd like to tell me?"

She pursed her lips. "I can't think of anything, but I'll let you know if there is."

"Thanks." Relieved that at least one person had been a genuine help, I stood. "I'll let you know if we have any updates."

She rose to her feet. "Interesting to meet you, Head Witch."

"Likewise."

At some point during our conversation, Tansy had gone outside, so I went looking for her. I caught sight of her familiar red tail outside Were's My Coffee?, next to Rowan and her own familiar.

"Hey." Rowan greeted me with a wave. "Sorry we didn't get the chance to talk earlier."

"I know the lunch shift is busy," I said. "You're probably wondering why I was talking to Gabriel again."

"Who?" she asked. "What I saw was you getting lunch with a guy who wasn't Harvey, but I figured there must be a reason."

I winced. I hadn't even thought of how it might have looked from an outside perspective. "Gabriel's the new guy on the Sky Hopper team, so I wanted to ask a few questions about Jansen's death."

"Did he know anything?"

"Nope, but I'm not sure he was telling the full truth about why Tomas seems to hate him so much." My phone buzzed. I checked my messages and found that Piper wanted to know if I was up for meeting at the Fox's Den. "Want to go and meet Piper at the Fox's Den? I can tell you the latest while we're there."

Perhaps not the best choice of meet-up spots, given the unfortunate end to my Friday night, but my love of the cosy pub and my desire to catch up with my friends won out over my apprehension at setting foot in the site of Jansen's murder.

Tansy poked me in the ankle. "I thought you were going to help me look for that magpie's nasty little traps in the forest."

Oops. "Want to come and plot with us as well? Between us, we should be able to come up with a better plan than walking around the woods until one of us falls into a net."

"Fine." Tansy remained in a subdued mood on the walk to the pub, so I made a mental note to make it up to her in the morning.

At the Fox's Den, Rowan and I picked out a table and waited for Piper to arrive. Once she did, I told them both what I'd seen at yesterday's practise session and then today's new developments, including my chat with Jansen's ex-wife.

"Wow," said Piper. "So the messages weren't blackmail, Jansen's ex-wife didn't know he was murdered, and the guy was in debt up to his elbows?"

"Essentially, yes." I sat back in my seat as our drinks appeared on the table in front of us. "I bet Harvey knew all about Jansen's spending habits and was having none of his excuses."

"Good for him." Piper took a sip of her bright-pink cocktail. "Your brother can't use those messages to accuse him of murder then."

"Are you sure his ex was telling the truth though?" asked Rowan. "She might have been lying through her teeth the entire time. Why come back to Wildwood Heath if she didn't expect to get something from the will?"

That part had struck a nerve with my cousin, I didn't doubt, because Rowan had almost missed out on her inheritance from Grandma thanks to her own mother's scheming. That didn't mean Jansen's ex-wife was the same though.

"It sounded like she had zero faith in Jansen to have left anything to her but debts," I replied. "She didn't seem that interested in Sky Hopper either, but not sharing interests isn't that unusual."

Their relationship might have been doomed to failure, but Jansen's death was a different matter entirely, and once again, it all came back to the Sky Hopper team.

We fell silent when a waiter passed by our table, and I wondered why the youngish shifter looked familiar for a moment before I recognised him as the same guy who'd been working at the bar the night of Jansen's death.

I rose to my feet, keeping an eye on the waiter's back. "One second. I'll be right back."

"What's she doing now?" Piper asked Rowan.

"Haven't a clue," Rowan responded.

The waiter saw me following him and halted in mid-step. "Oh… Head Witch?"

"Hey," I said. "Sorry about the other night."

"Yeah… I've thrown out plenty of drunk shifters, but nobody's ever dropped dead in here before."

"No kidding." I chose my words carefully. "I wondered… do you remember the guy sitting next to the bar that night? The one whose head was covered in bandages?"

The shifter turned to properly face me. "Hard to forget him, considering he looked dead on his feet. What about him?"

"This is a weird question, but did you notice a badge on the table in front of him?"

"A badge?" he echoed.

"Yeah, about this big." I measured the size of the badge between my fingers. "A silver badge in the shape of a bird."

"Oh, one of those Sky Hopper mascots? Yeah, he did."

Well, well. My brother might have reason to question Tomas again after all. "Also, did you notice the guy with the bandages acting oddly during the party?"

"Aside from sitting at the bar while everyone else was celebrating?" He shook his head. "I wasn't paying too much attention. He didn't seem to want to talk to anyone. He was messing around on his phone the whole evening instead."

Hmm. I wondered if the police had checked *his* phone. "Even when Jansen died? Did you see how he reacted?"

He flinched. "I was too busy calling the police to pay any attention, to be honest."

"Thanks for telling me."

I returned to the table, where both Piper and Rowan watched me in bemusement.

"What was that about?" Piper asked.

"That guy was working at the bar the night of the party," I explained. "And the person who is currently my number-one suspect happened to be sitting directly in front of him, possibly with the murder weapon right there on the table."

"Seriously?" said Rowan. "Are you going to tell your brother?"

"You can count on it."

11

As it turned out, I didn't have to wait until the morning to speak to Ramsey. I left the pub with plenty of time to get enough sleep before another day at the office and walked home with Tansy. Her mood had improved after I'd renewed my promise to help her hunt for traps in the forest tomorrow, but frankly, I didn't have a clue how I'd fit that in between juggling my job as Head Witch and trying to prove Harvey's innocence.

After quietly unlocking the door and entering the house, I assumed I was alone downstairs until a voice spoke from the shadows of the living room. "Robin."

I nearly jumped out of my skin. "Ramsey?"

As I walked into the living room, he leaned forwards from where he sat on the sofa in the darkness. "Sorry I startled you."

I squinted at him. "Why are you sitting in the dark?"

He looked slightly rumpled, and an empty beer can lay

next to him, along with another on the floor. *What's up with him?*

"Nothing," he answered.

"Have you been drinking?"

"I thought that's what *you* were doing."

"No... well, only one drink. I have to go to work tomorrow, and I thought you did too."

"Yes, I do. Or rather, I don't." He slumped back against the cushions. "My coworkers think I should take a day off, but I can't leave this case unattended."

"No more clues on Jansen's murder?"

He grunted, which meant yes. It was rare enough that he actually admitted to having difficulties that I found myself staring at him for a moment.

"What?" he said defensively. "It's hardly the first time. A fair proportion of homicides go unsolved."

Did he expect me to gloat? Hardly. If it took a minor breakdown to finally convince him to let me help out, I'd take it. Anything to spare Harvey from being jailed.

"Just surprised you'd admit it." I moved the beer can aside and sat down next to him on the sofa. "Is there anything in particular bugging you? Sometimes you need an outside opinion to get perspective."

He gave me a sideways look. "You're hardly an outside opinion, Robin, considering you're trying to defend one of the suspects."

"Everyone has their biases one way or another."

Like his own bias *against* said suspect.

His eyes narrowed, then he exhaled in a sigh. "I suppose you're right. The thing that's bugging me is that nothing is bloody adding up."

I blinked. "That's not very specific. You mean the

evidence? Or is everyone throwing accusations at each other but none of them making much sense?"

"Nobody has made an accusation," he said. "If anything, they're doing the opposite and outright avoiding accusing anyone at all."

"Not even Tomas?" I asked. "I thought he hated Gabriel being on the team."

"If he does, he didn't accuse him of murder."

Gabriel seemed to think otherwise, and Tomas's outright bullying during their practise session implied more than a strong dislike... but perhaps he hadn't got up the courage to actually come out and make the accusation. Or he'd hoped the police would come to the conclusion themselves—which might have been the case if Ramsey hadn't been focused on Harvey instead of him.

"Have you looked at the photos yet?" I asked.

"Yes, and I gave them to my colleagues to examine in more depth."

"And?" I pressed. "Did you have a look at the badge on the table next to Tomas? Because I asked the bartender who worked at the Fox's Den the night of the party, and he confirmed that it *was* a badge belonging to a Sky Hopper player."

"You went back to the Fox's Den?" He sat upright. "Not with *him*."

"Not with Harvey, no." The brief spark of sympathy inside me began to dim. "I went with Piper and Rowan. Anyway, I saw that the same guy was working at the bar, so I asked him, and he confirmed the badge that killed Jansen was right in front of Tomas. Isn't that worth another look?"

"You aren't going to let this drop, are you?"

"No, because Tomas had the murder weapon. He was also on his phone all night, according to Gabriel. Have you checked *his* messages?"

"I see your point," he said grudgingly. "I will mention that to my teammates."

Sorted. "What did Harvey actually say about the messages he and Jansen supposedly sent one another, anyway? If he didn't deny sending them, he couldn't have believed he had anything to hide."

"He mentioned having an argument with Jansen, but he didn't recall the details," he said, sounding unconvinced. "He also claimed that Jansen never intended to leave town and that his claim that he planned to play for another team was an empty threat."

"That's true." Should I tell him I'd already spoken to Jansen's ex-wife, or would that only stop him from opening up to me entirely? "Jansen was retiring. It would make no sense for him to suddenly pack his bags and go to join another team. Also, he was in debt, so letting him run amok with the team's money wouldn't have been a good idea. Harvey was only looking out for the rest of the team."

"Did he tell you that?"

"No, I worked it out. Don't look at me like that. I've been with Piper and Rowan all evening, and since you have his phone, I can't have messaged him, can I?"

He merely grunted in answer. "I'll think on it a little more."

"Do that." *Please.* Harvey was innocent, and Tomas couldn't have looked guiltier if he had a neon sign floating above his head proclaiming him as the murderer. "What's the plan for tomorrow?"

"I have an appointment to speak to Jansen's ex-wife, for a start," he said. "Then I'll have another look at what I've gathered from the other team members. I have no intention of arresting anyone for the moment."

That was a start. If he was at least beginning to entertain the possibility that Harvey wasn't the culprit, then I'd achieved one victory.

I rose to my feet. "And if I were to show up at the police station and offer my assistance again, you wouldn't throw me out?"

"No. Happy?"

I grinned. "That's all I wanted to hear."

———

I woke up abruptly when Tansy jumped on my face. "Ow. What are you doing?"

"Waking you up." She prodded me in the cheekbone. "Whatever happened to finding those traps?"

I groaned. "Wait."

Tansy walked over my chin, her tail flicking me in the nose, before hopping onto my chest. "I'm sitting here until you get up."

"All right, all right." I swatted her off me so I could climb out of bed and get dressed. I *had* forgotten that I'd promised to help her find evidence of Aunt Shannon's trickery, but between being Head Witch and trying to prove Harvey's innocence, free daylight hours were in short supply. Which was probably why Tansy had woken me at the crack of dawn.

Resigned to yet another day of dozing off at the office, I headed downstairs with my sceptre in my hand. Then I followed Tansy out the back door and made my way through the garden, past the carefully arranged flower beds and the array of wildlife clustering around the bird feeders. It was early enough that Piper hadn't come over to water the flowers and trim the rosebushes yet, and all was quiet when we reached the path winding through the forest.

A glance over Aunt Shannon's fence showed no signs of her or her scheming magpie familiar.

"Tansy, where did you find the trap?"

"There." She pointed with her tail to the back of Aunt Shannon's garden. "It was attached to the fence."

I examined the fence closely and found part of the sticky webbing still attached. Catching the end of a thread between my fingertips, I tugged at the webbing until it came detached, at which point I put it in my pocket to keep from accidentally gluing my fingers together.

Tansy peered up at the fence and recoiled. "The scoundrel. Look at the gate."

I followed her gaze to the back gate leading into Aunt Shannon's garden and found that the wooden surface was covered in the same sticky substance. "Guess she upgraded her security. I don't know that I can call her out on what she chooses to do to her own fence though, because she'd claim she's within her rights to protect her own house."

Never mind that she violated Rowan's privacy on a regular basis herself.

Tansy's tail wagged. "That's not what she's doing. She wants a fight, and I want to give her one."

"Then go and beat up some pigeons. Come on, you don't actually want to start a fight with Myrtle, do you?"

"I'd win," she informed me. "You know I would."

"Sure, but I don't want you to get hurt." I glared at the back of Aunt Shannon's house. "We'll tell Rowan first. If anyone deserves to throw the first punch, it's her."

Not that Rowan *wanted* anything to do with her mother, but if Myrtle showed her face at the coffee shop again, perhaps we needed to concoct a trap of our own.

———

The morning dragged while I watched the clock out of the corner of my eye and counted down the hours until my lunch break. Then I'd be able to talk to Rowan, but first of all, I intended to drop by the police station and find out if they'd spoken to Tomas yet. I'd had no opportunity to speak to Harvey in the meantime, and he hadn't sent me any messages either... probably because my brother had confiscated his mobile phone.

Okay, I really need to get him off the suspect list. And fast.

Lunchtime arrived. Once I'd escaped my office, I speed-walked down the high street to the police station and entered via the automatic doors. The rest of the staff were so used to seeing me around by this point that nobody challenged me on my way in.

Ramsey, though, looked down at me as if I'd left a trail of mud all over the lobby. "Robin, I thought you'd come after work, not now."

"I have time." Not much of it, admittedly, but I had even less patience left. "I just wanted to find out how the questioning is going."

"Slowly." Ramsey might have been back to his usual stern self, but he looked even more tired than the previous day, if possible. "I spoke to Jansen's ex-wife, and what she told me complicated the evidence."

"Really?" He didn't know I'd spoken to her yesterday, and I preferred to keep it that way, so I refrained from mentioning that we'd already talked to one another. "Complicated it in what way?"

"She confirmed that Jansen has a history of debt."

"How does that complicate anything?" I asked. "Doesn't it confirm what I said yesterday about Harvey looking out for the team by taking control over their finances so Jansen couldn't spend every penny?"

"We still only have his word as proof," he said, "and the rest of the team knows nothing about the messages they sent to one another."

"So you spoke to the other team members?" I gave him an assessing look. "Like Tomas?"

"Not yet," he replied. "He wasn't free until this afternoon."

That figured. "I thought you were going to make him a priority, considering the badge that Jansen choked on was right in front of his nose."

"I intend to ask him some questions, but there's no way to verify that it was definitely the same badge, nor that he was the one who used it to commit murder," said Ramsey. "My team is still going through the other members' correspondence—and your photos, Robin."

So much for an easy way to a solution. "I take it you aren't going to let them meet up for their next practise session? Isn't that today?"

His brows shot up. "That's not my choice, but I imagine the captain will want to postpone the session until the case is closed."

"If he's here, may I talk to him?" I asked. "The captain, I mean?"

He gave me a suspicious stare. "About what?"

"I just want to know how he is. Since, you know, he can't text me at the moment."

"You don't make this easy, do you?" His shoulders slumped just a little, and he pointed me towards the waiting room. "He's in there."

Heart drumming against my rib cage, I approached the door and spotted Harvey sitting on one of the uncomfortable metal chairs through the glass topping the door. He rose to his feet when I entered the room. "Robin?"

"That's me." He was also alone in the waiting room, an unexpected bonus to an otherwise grim situation. "I'd have texted you, but you know."

"Yeah." His expression dimmed. "I had to cancel this evening's practise session, and it's been hard to let the rest of the team know without access to my phone."

"Want me to tell them instead?" I offered.

"I've already told most of them," he said. "Except Gabriel, since I haven't seen him at the station today."

If he hadn't been here, then I assumed it meant the police didn't consider him a suspect. Our conversation the previous day came to mind, along with a rush of suspicion, but it was beyond me to tell how truthful he'd been when he'd claimed not to have known the rest of the team prior to Jansen's death. I didn't see him as a murderer, not least because he'd been nowhere near where the badge had been when Jansen had died. Yet there was something slightly off about his explanation for Tomas's irrational animosity towards him that I couldn't quite put my finger on. Tomas himself had better show up for his questioning later this afternoon.

I glanced over my shoulder to make sure nobody was listening to us talking and dropped my voice. "I was worried when I heard about the messages that showed up on Jansen's phone."

Harvey's expression clouded. "I never thought they'd be taken out of context like that."

"So you did know about his issues with finances?"

"I did," he confirmed. "Extensively, I'm afraid. It was my responsibility to make sure he didn't spend all the team's money, so I did have to be firm with him some-times. I have to admit I was worried about what he'd do when he retired. He was in enough debt already."

I turned this over in my mind. "Who handled the team's finances before you became captain then?"

"It varied, but when I joined the team, Casey was in charge of the finances," he answered. "Then when he left the team, I took over from him."

Casey. He hadn't been called back for questioning, as far as I was aware, but might he know something the others didn't?

"I didn't realise Casey had that level of responsibility," I remarked. "Before he quit. Did he and Jansen get on well?"

"They did, which is why Casey was happy to deal with the financial side of running the team and prevent word from getting out about Jansen's difficulties."

"So the rest of the team don't know?"

"They've probably figured it out by now," he said. "Jansen and I occasionally came into conflict over it, including in those messages your brother found, but he always regretted blowing up at me after he'd calmed down."

"Do you know…" I faltered, not willing to mention the photos of Tomas in case it caused the police to assume we'd concocted the plan together. "I mean, it seems weird that the killer chose to use one of the spare captain's badges to commit murder. I know the badges used to be Jansen's, but might someone have wanted to make *you* look guilty?"

That was one theory I hadn't delved into yet… that someone was trying to pin the blame on the captain. Gabriel seemed to think that *he'd* been likely to get blamed, but that made little sense given that the rest of the team had been much closer to Jansen than the newcomer had. The captain though?

A worried expression came over Harvey's face. "I can't think of anyone who'd have a reason to. Certainly nobody on the team, anyway."

Hmm. Tomas's unpleasant attitude seemed to extend to the captain, but it'd been Gabriel who'd been the primary target of his ire. "I guess it's bad luck that the police found those messages. What about his ex-wife? I bet they used to have the same arguments."

"Not recently though," he said. "I did wonder why she came back to Wildwood Heath, but by all accounts, she didn't even know he was murdered until she got here. I gather they haven't spoken recently."

"She claimed she wanted to find out how he'd died," I explained. "Since the police didn't give her the details over the phone."

"I can see why she might have got curious," he allowed. "No, I don't think she was involved in his death, but we don't know one another well enough for her word to be enough to convince the police of my innocence."

"Who might be able to back you up then? Casey?"

"I don't think he wants anything to do with us, to be honest." He grimaced. "Since he left the team, he's been working at the Mermaid's Meadow."

"The nightclub." The Mermaid's Meadow wouldn't open until later that evening, but I didn't have long before I needed to get back to work anyway. "I have to go. I'm sorry, Harvey."

He gave me a strained smile. "Really, don't worry about me. I'll be fine."

Apparently, I didn't look convinced. He leaned forwards and touched my shoulder, eliciting a fluttering sensation in my chest that made me severely regret that my brother was waiting on the other side of the door, no doubt watching to make sure we didn't get up to any mischief. Why could nothing in my life be simple?

Sure enough, I walked out of the room and found Ramsey waiting on the other side of the door.

"Heading back to the office?" he asked.

"Yes," I told him. "When are you going to give Harvey his phone back?"

"When we've verified whether there are any other messages that give us cause for suspicion," he answered. "I know you're impatient for this to be over, but I have to follow protocol."

I might have commented that his penchant for sticking to protocol had caused more problems than it'd solved, but instead, I said, "Thanks for letting me talk to him."

Once I'd left the police station, I bought a sandwich

from Were's My Coffee? to take back to the office with me.

On my way out the door, Tansy jumped on my shoulder from the drainpipe, startling me. "Look up there!"

I tilted my head back, seeing a flutter of black-and-white wings take off from the window of the upper floor. Rowan's room, to be precise.

That bloody magpie.

"I know it's her!" Tansy exclaimed. "She *was* spying on Rowan."

"Thought so." Rowan herself wasn't on her shift at the moment, so I could only assume she was oblivious to her unwanted visitor. "Tansy, can you climb up there and make sure she didn't get into the room?"

"Hang on." She scurried up the drainpipe, while I waited a minute for her to return. "Nope. The window's closed."

"Good. Next time, we need to get proof." I reached into my pocket for what was left of the trap, but it'd mostly lost its stickiness by this point. "Or use another one of these to catch her in the act."

In fact, Rowan would be within *her* rights to set up a trap on the window to catch any unwanted intruders.

Tansy cackled. "We'll set up our own trap that she won't forget in a hurry."

"Exactly." I might not have managed to spare Harvey from a future behind bars yet, but if anyone deserved to have a worse week than mine, it was Aunt Shannon. "We'll get her. Count on it."

12

The rest of the afternoon at work dragged as if I was trying to fly a weighted broomstick. At least I didn't have any meetings to deal with, because pretending to be friendly to Aunt Shannon was as appealing as playing Sky Hopper in a storm.

Grandma seemed to have given up on giving me lessons on using the sceptre altogether, which was probably for the best. That left me with nothing but paperwork, plus the occasional visit from Mum to dump another task or three on my head. She didn't ask about the investigation, luckily, because I had nothing to say on the matter except for an incoherent noise of frustration—as Chloe found out when she made the mistake of asking how I was doing.

"Rough week?" she asked sympathetically.

"Eh." I shrugged. "Not as bad as some, but frustrating."

"Let me know if there's anything I can take off your hands."

"Honestly, you've taken enough off my hands," I told

her. "If you do any more, I'll have to crown you as Head Witch in my place."

Chloe gave a smile. "No, I prefer a behind-the-scenes role."

Same here, believe me. As far as assistants went, Mum had chosen well, and I was glad to have Chloe to help me navigate the treacherous waters of being Head Witch. I wouldn't drag her into my rivalries with Aunt Shannon though, nor my attempts to convince my brother of Harvey's innocence. At least I had a reprieve from meeting the other Head Witches for now, because I couldn't imagine having to deal with *that* on top of the rest of this crap.

Tansy came into my office as the workday came to an end. "Ready to go?"

Meaning: Was I ready to talk to Rowan about setting up a trap for a certain magpie? "What if Myrtle's already there?"

"I'll grab her before she can sneak off." Tansy ran ahead of me, her bushy red tail waving in anticipation.

I speed-walked to the café and found Rowan finishing her shift. Once I'd explained our plan, she was on board right away.

"I'll ask my tarantulas to leave webbing all over the window and use a spell to make it extra sticky," Rowan said. "That ought to get her."

"Awesome." I checked the time. "Will the Mermaid's Meadow be open now, do you know?"

"The nightclub?" Rowan frowned at me. "Don't you have work tomorrow?"

"I'm not going clubbing, but someone who works

there might be able to help me defend Harvey against the accusations."

"Oh." She nodded in understanding. "I think it'll be opening for the evening, but I've never been there. My sister likes it too much."

"Ugh." I hadn't known clubbing was Vanessa's thing. "I'll let you know how I get on."

I didn't know if Casey would be at the nightclub at this time, but it was worth a look around. The Mermaid's Meadow lay down an unappealing side street, a brick building decorated with motifs of dancing mermaids. I'd never been there before, preferring cosy pubs to noisy crowds, and while it might have been different at night, the place was downright grimy during the day. I nudged the faded wooden door open with my heel, and my feet immediately stuck to the floor when I entered the nightclub.

Tansy wrinkled her nose. "I'm not going in there. Come and let me know how it goes."

"I won't be long." Peeling my shoe from the floor, I picked my way across to the dusty bar, having to squint to see where I was going. I assumed the strobe lights would come blazing on at night, but during the day, the place resembled a cave. It wasn't until I reached the bar that I saw Casey standing on a ladder nearby, reattaching one of the glow-in-the-dark mermaid motifs which had come loose from the ceiling.

Upon spotting me, he scowled. "You again?"

"Can I talk to you?" I trod towards him before he could descend the ladder and escape the way he had outside the café. "It's important."

"If you want me to save that Sky Hopper team, then

you can forget it," he said. "I don't care what happens to any of them."

Typical. "Look, can you just answer a couple of questions? I heard you used to handle the team's finances before you quit. Is that true?"

He gave me a suspicious stare. "Harvey told you that?"

"Yes, he did. I assume you were aware of Jansen's issues with handling cash?"

"That's putting it mildly," he scoffed. "He was a walking disaster. He'd have bankrupted the entire team if he'd been allowed to handle the finances himself. I did all that for him for years. And what gratitude did I get? They gave me the shaft."

I frowned. "Was it him who kicked you off the team?"

"Nobody kicked me off the team." He jumped off the ladder. "I quit."

Harvey had said he and Jansen had got along well… but I'd never asked him *why* Casey had walked away from the team. "Why?"

He made for the door to the back room. Quick as a flash, I wedged my foot in the doorway to prevent him from closing it. "If you won't answer my questions, I'll send my brother instead. I'm trying to stop an innocent man going to jail."

He snorted. "Innocent? Hardly."

"What's your problem with Harvey?"

"Harvey?" His brow furrowed. "Never said I had an issue with him."

"He's at the top of the suspect list, Casey. I think we both know that he can't be the murderer, so who is it?"

"You think I know?" He shook his head. "I'm years

behind on the team's drama, and frankly, I don't miss it in the slightest."

"Then why'd you quit?" I asked. "Who was ungrateful towards you, exactly?"

He shrugged. "Everyone, in a way. It wasn't worth the hassle in the end."

"Was Tomas always a bully?"

"Tomas?" A moment passed. "Yeah, I never liked that guy."

"I don't think anyone else does, either," I remarked. "The others said he's just having a bad week, but the way he was acting at the party makes me think otherwise."

"You think he killed Jansen?" He blinked in surprise. "Your guess is as good as mine. I wasn't there; I was serving cheap cocktails to academy students."

Hmm. "I'm actually close to proving that Tomas killed Jansen, but I need support. Would you be willing to back me up?"

Casey firmly shook his head. "I'm not getting involved. No way."

I should have seen that one coming. "Tomas is the killer, I'm sure, but nobody will hear a word against him. Except for Gabriel, but he's the main target for his bullying…"

I trailed off as an odd look came over him. "Gabriel? Scrawny kid who looks like a stiff breeze could blow him away… *that* Gabriel?"

"Yes… why?"

"They let him onto the team?" He gave a wild kind of laugh. "Oh, *now* I get it."

"I don't." What was he talking about? "Did you know Gabriel?"

"Not personally, but everyone knew about the incident when he got caught cheating at the regional Sky Hopper championship tryouts a few years ago."

"Cheating?" He'd been involved in cheating at Sky Hopper… and they'd let him onto the team anyway?

"You don't know?" He raised a brow. "I would have thought that would have come out when the police started their questioning, unless the rest of the team didn't know. Jansen certainly did though."

"Why would he pick him for the team anyway?" No wonder Gabriel had been reluctant to admit if anyone on the team had known him prior to joining… but was that why he'd assumed he'd be blamed for Jansen's death?

Unless… did he think the killer had been trying to get him kicked off the team?

"You think I know?" Casey scoffed. "Maybe Jansen thought he turned over a new leaf. I don't know or care, but evidently, someone did."

Like Tomas. Was his bullying Gabriel an indirect form of revenge? Or a distraction from his *real* revenge, in murdering Jansen and disgracing Gabriel in the process? Either was possible, but I didn't have the faintest idea if the police were aware of Gabriel's history. If I told them myself, would it make Harvey look any less guilty? I didn't know, but there must be evidence of Gabriel's history of cheating online somewhere. That kind of thing was hard to keep quiet.

This time, when Casey entered the back room, I didn't try to follow. Instead, I left the Mermaid's Meadow, my feet sticking with every step. Tansy waited at the door, and I gave her the rundown on our way to the police station.

I knocked on Ramsey's office door, and he answered with his usual long-suffering expression. "What is it now?"

"I spoke to Casey and found out something I think you'll want to know."

His jaw twitched. "This has better be good. Casey is already off the suspect list."

"It's not him. The information concerns their newest player, Gabriel, who was once involved in an incident which involved cheating in a Sky Hopper game. Before he joined the team, that is. It's possible that someone objected to Jansen letting him join and decided to take matters into their own hands."

"Can anyone confirm this?"

Good question. "I'm not sure if the rest of the team knows, but if you search the Wizarding Web, it's bound to have been reported somewhere."

He exhaled. "We've already conducted the day's interviews. Let me think."

"Where's Harvey then?"

"He left several hours ago, so I assume he went home."

Without his phone, I guessed. "What did Tomas say when you questioned him? Did you ask about the badge?"

"He denied all involvement in Jansen's death," he replied. "Again."

"If Tomas knew about Gabriel's past, it would explain why he was treating him so badly." That must be it. "And if he got mad at Jansen for hiring him, I can see it being a motive for murder."

Ramsey didn't look convinced. "When did this happen, precisely?"

"A couple of years ago, I think." Tomas might have

followed the news and refused to believe Gabriel had truly learned from his mistakes. That much was obvious.

Ramsey pulled out his phone. "I'll call your friend and ask him to come into the office again."

"What—Harvey?" How'd he manage to get to *him* from my revelations about Gabriel's history? "Why? What's he got to do with any of this?"

"As the current captain and the person in charge of the team's finances, he has responsibility for his teammates," said Ramsey. "If it turns out *he* knew his player's history, then it's relevant."

Oh, boy. Harvey would have told the police if he knew, right? "Would it matter? He respected Jansen's decision to appoint Gabriel as his replacement. Even if he did know Gabriel had a history of cheating, then it shouldn't make a difference."

"Given the timing of his argument with Jansen, it might."

This wasn't supposed to happen. Perhaps I should have dragged Ramsey to talk to Casey instead or otherwise pressured him to take Harvey's side, but instead, I'd unintentionally painted a target on Harvey's head again.

Several tense minutes passed before Harvey showed up at the police station, his brows rising at the sight of me standing next to my brother in the lobby. "Something wrong?"

"We found new information about one of the players," I explained. "For some reason, Ramsey wants to confirm the details with you before speaking to the affected parties."

"I thought it prudent to speak to the captain first." Ramsey beckoned both of us to follow him into his office.

A rarity, and a sign that he was taking my concerns seriously… but why did he have to drag Harvey into this mess?

Harvey entered the office, his gaze taking in the neat desk and Prickles sitting on top of the wooden surface. "What information? Which player?"

Ramsey faced him. "We have recently been told that Gabriel was involved in an incident in which he was caught cheating in a Sky Hopper game."

Harvey's posture stiffened. "He told you that? Gabriel did?"

"No… Casey," I said. "Did you know?"

Oh, no. He did know. I should have guessed that nothing would have escaped the captain's attention.

Harvey's gaze slid to my brother. "Jansen convinced me to let him try out for the team anyway. He told me Gabriel regretted his decision and that he'd changed, so I decided to trust him. We put the matter behind us."

"Tomas didn't," I blurted, desperate to steer my brother's attention back onto Tomas instead of Harvey. "That's why he bullied Gabriel so relentlessly. Isn't it?"

"That doesn't mean he would ever hurt Jansen." Harvey didn't meet my eyes. "I'm sorry, Robin. I know you want this solved, but Tomas… I don't think he's the killer."

I gave Ramsey a pleading look. I understood Harvey's need to protect his friends and teammates, but Tomas had every reason to have murdered Jansen, and each piece of new information only served to make him look guiltier.

My brother addressed Harvey. "Thank you for your input. You can go."

I stepped in. "Aren't you going to call Tomas in for

questioning?"

"We already spoke to him today," Ramsey said. "I'll add his name to tomorrow's list, but I can't say this information makes him any likelier to be the murderer."

I opened my mouth to argue, but Harvey put a hand on my arm, startling me into silence. "I would prefer it if none of my teammates is arrested. I'll see you later, okay?"

Harvey didn't wait for a reply. When the door closed, leaving my brother and me alone in his office, Ramsey exhaled and looked up at me. "That was instructive."

My face heated. "I thought he didn't know."

"Sorry, Robin," he said. "If it helps, I don't think Tomas looks innocent either, but Harvey seems determined to defend him, and I have to treat everyone fairly."

I said nothing, wishing I'd just hit Tomas over the head with the sceptre at the practise session instead of letting him walk away. I would have bet he'd have been quick to show his true colours then.

As entertaining as the thought might have been, I couldn't shake the sinking feeling that I might just have screwed up my chance at a relationship with Harvey on top of everything else.

With nothing to do but return home, I retreated from the police station. Tansy hopped onto my shoulder and wrapped her tail around my neck in a comforting manner.

"You haven't checked with Rowan about whether she caught her spy yet," she murmured in my ear.

"She said she'd message me if she caught that magpie," I recalled. "I guess Myrtle's lying low. I'm not really in the mood to confront Aunt Shannon anyway, to tell you the truth."

Tansy jumped off my shoulder. "Then I'll do it for you."

I suppressed a groan as she took off like a rocket down the high street. I didn't catch up to her until she vanished down the nearest route to the woodland path, and at that point, I figured it couldn't hurt to have another poke around. At least the forest was peaceful and didn't judge me for my recent mistakes, but even the tranquil sound of birdsong didn't drown out the voices in the back of my mind whispering that I'd blown my chances with Harvey altogether.

When we reached the back of Aunt Shannon's house, I let Tansy take the lead. "Be careful."

Tansy scampered along a branch overlooking the fence and stood on her hind legs, her tail bristling. A rustling noise came from the other side of the fence at the back of Aunt Shannon's garden. *Who's that?*

I approached the fence, taking care not to touch the sticky webbing covering the top, and found myself looking down at my cousin Vanessa. "What are you doing lurking in the bushes?"

"It's my house," she said haughtily. "I can do whatever I like. What are *you* doing in my garden?"

"I'm not in your garden." I gestured at the fence. "I was admiring your decorations. What's with the spiderwebs? Or whatever it is?"

"My mother wanted to ward off intruders."

"Really, now." More rustling sounded. What *was* she doing down there? I stood on tiptoe to peer into the bushes and saw the wand in her hand the moment before she pointed it at me.

On instinct, I raised the sceptre and cast a boundary

charm the same instant her wand went off. Her spell bounced straight off an invisible shield and rebounded into her face. Vanessa shrank into the bush, disappearing from sight.

"What did she get hit with?" I asked. "Tansy, is she in one piece?"

Tansy trod along the branch to peer into the garden. "Yes, but I think she's a frog. Or invisible, but there's definitely a frog down there."

"A frog?" Seriously? *That* was the spell she'd been casting on me? "A pig would have been more appropriate."

Tansy laughed so hard that she nearly fell off the branch. "Excellent. I hope her familiar eats her."

"I wouldn't go that far." I reached over the fence and plucked the frog out of the bush, and Vanessa promptly slid free of my hands like a piece of soap. "Stop running unless you want to get caught in the web."

Tansy snickered. "Wouldn't be a tragedy though, would it?"

"Honestly." I reached into my pocket for the remaining thread of the spiderweb trap and used it to bind Vanessa's feet together. She croaked at full volume, unable to hop away.

I pointed the sceptre at her, and she cringed back. *Hmm. Maybe using another spell isn't the best approach.* Besides, if I turned her back into a human, she'd make a swift getaway.

I scooped her up in my hand again. "Let's see what the leader of the Wildwood Coven has to say about you trying to turn the Head Witch into a frog."

13

"What have you done?" Mum faced me over the kitchen table, where I'd put down the unfortunate frog. Vanessa flailed and kicked, unable to free her feet from the sticky webbing.

"Deflected her own spell in her face," I explained. "Turning people into frogs is hardly imaginative enough to be one of my spells."

Tansy cackled with laughter, sounding more like a raven than a squirrel. At least her mood had improved, as had mine—though the shadow of what I'd done to Harvey hovered over my head like a storm cloud.

"What were you doing out there in the first place?" Mum wanted to know.

"I found Vanessa hiding in the bushes at the back of her garden," I said. "When I asked what she was doing, she flipped out and tried to hex me."

Vanessa let out an indignant croak, no doubt wanting to protest, but I hadn't lied, and it was entirely her own fault she'd ended up in that state to begin with.

"Her delightful mother has also been putting some sticky traps on the back of their fence to catch any unfortunate animals who try to get into the garden," added Tansy.

"You mean familiars." Mum's expression suggested she'd already guessed that Tansy had first discovered the traps the hard way. "I thought you were going to leave your Aunt Shannon alone—both of you."

"Her familiar has been spying on Rowan behind her back," I told her. "Tansy followed her home from the café and found her traps."

Mum tutted. "It doesn't surprise me, but she's within her rights to set up all the traps she likes in her own garden."

"The wildlife in the forest would beg to differ," I said. "Also, spying on Rowan and then using those traps on anyone who tries to catch her familiar in the act isn't playing fair. Let alone whatever Vanessa was doing."

Vanessa gave a pitiful croak.

Mum considered the frog. "Leaving her like that overnight is out of the question. Carmilla might eat her."

I snorted. "Serve her right."

"Hear, hear," said Tansy.

Mum gave me a look. "I really thought this was behind us."

"Don't blame me. Blame the frog princess over there."

Vanessa croaked balefully at both of us. If we *did* leave her like that, there was no telling what Aunt Shannon would do in return. I still hadn't dealt with her apparent obsession with spying on Rowan, either.

I rolled my eyes. "I'll try to turn her back, but I should probably do it outside."

"I'd rather leave her like that," Tansy ventured.

I would have liked to, too, but I didn't want her lurking in the house either, especially if she overheard us discussing Jansen's murder and Harvey's potential upcoming arrest. Assuming the other side of my family didn't already know, of course.

I reached down to pick up Vanessa. She croaked in alarm and tried to hop away, but Tansy swatted her backwards and caused her to trip over the end of the thread binding her feet together.

"Calm down. I'm going to turn you back." I managed to get both hands around her slippery frog form and then carried her out the front door.

Placing her on the doorstep, I pointed the sceptre directly at the cowering frog. "A reversal spell should do the trick."

I waved the sceptre, and a puff of smoke filled the air. A second later, Vanessa lay in a crumpled heap next to the doorstep, a pile of what appeared to be business cards adorned with cartoon mermaids at her feet.

"You'll pay for that."

"It was your spell," I countered. "Why *did* you try to hex me?"

She scrambled to her feet. "Because you were about to hex *me*."

"No, I really wasn't." Was she really that paranoid? Possibly, yes. "What's with the glittery mermaid business cards?"

Evidently, they'd fallen out of her pockets when she'd landed in a heap on the floor. A flush lit up her cheeks, and she gathered them up with shaking hands. "I got them from the Mermaid's Meadow the other night. They were doing a themed event where you could exchange one card for a free drink."

How'd she get that many? Stole them from the other patrons, probably.

I jabbed a finger towards the house next door. "Go on, and if you want to tell your mother I hexed you, then you can tell her to leave Rowan alone while you're at it."

Shooting me a venomous look, Vanessa marched towards her own house with all the dignity she could muster.

I rolled my eyes and returned to the hall, firmly closing the door behind me. "That's that sorted then."

Tansy scampered ahead of me into the living room, where Mum had returned to the sofa with a stack of paperwork.

"Where did you go after work, anyway?" Mum asked. "You're not still 'helping' Ramsey with his investigation?"

Should I tell her? I didn't need to deal with her judgement on top of Ramsey's, but I could hardly screw up any more badly than I already had. "Yeah... but it didn't exactly work out the way I hoped."

In brief terms, I told her about the Sky Hopper team's convoluted history, from Jansen's spending habits to Gabriel's apparent history of cheating at sports. I also mentioned the photos I'd snapped of the party and how Ramsey had refused to take them seriously as evidence against Tomas, adding that Harvey hadn't helped matters by refusing to hear a word against any of his players.

"You should have guessed that Harvey knew about his new teammate's history," Mum said. "Jansen told him everything, didn't he?"

"Yeah, and it was public knowledge." In hindsight, I

shouldn't have been surprised. "I just don't understand why Harvey is going out of his way to defend Tomas. Even if he has good reasons for bullying Gabriel, he wrecked their last practise session for everyone else too. And then there's the fact that the badge Jansen choked to death on was right in front of his nose."

"Ramsey did look at the photos, didn't he?"

"Briefly, but I don't think they're a priority." I exhaled in a sigh. "He's been fixated on Harvey's text messages instead, because of that argument he and Jansen had, and now Gabriel's history as a cheater has captured his attention. Never mind that Harvey couldn't have held it against him if he agreed to give him the position."

"I understand that you're frustrated, Robin, but Ramsey is doing his best," Mum said. "You should focus on your job too. I heard from my mother that you're still struggling to use the sceptre."

"I'm not struggling to *use* it. I just don't think learning to cast every single spell in existence at a thousand times the volume is an efficient use of my time. Look at what I did to Vanessa."

"Nevertheless, you can't afford to get distracted from your duties, and it's only a matter of time before you're going to have to make a decision on where to put your focus."

In other words, I had no time for romance, least of all with someone who might be facing a future behind bars. "I think Ramsey is the person who needs reminding that he doesn't have to do it all himself, not me. I told him myself, but he never listens to a word I say."

"He does," she said. "Eventually. I wouldn't give up just yet, Robin."

Was *Mum* of all people giving me a pep talk? It was an improvement on being lectured, if nothing else, but before I could formulate a reply, a knock came from the front door.

Oh, no. I could guess who'd come to grace us with her presence.

Rising to her feet, Mum went to answer the door.

"I want to speak to the Head Witch." Aunt Shannon's voice drifted in from the hallway.

"Here." I stepped into view, to be greeted with the identical scowls of Aunt Shannon and Vanessa. "If you're going to reprimand me for turning your daughter into a frog, then I'll point out that it was her own spell that did it."

"She told me that you ambushed her."

"I found her hiding in the bushes in her own garden," I corrected. "No ambushing was involved."

"Your familiar was sniffing around the place," Vanessa said accusingly.

"Speaking of familiars, is yours ever going to leave Rowan alone?" I directed my question at Aunt Shannon. "I know she's spying on her and reporting back to you."

"Rowan turned her back on her own family. I can't have her getting up to any mischief behind our backs, can I?"

She wasn't even going to deny it? I supposed it was a little better than lying, but I'd had about enough of the pair of them. "You're paranoid."

"And you're a terrible Head Witch," Vanessa retaliated. "Isn't she, Mum?"

I stifled a laugh. "Is that really the best comeback you had available? Whether you're spying on your estranged family members or not has absolutely nothing to do with my own suitability for the position of Head Witch."

"You're an example of how far we've fallen." Aunt Shannon shook her head. "Though perhaps it's understandable that something as simple as one's brother arresting one's boyfriend would distract you from your job."

My heart sank into my shoes. "Ramsey hasn't arrested anyone."

Aunt Shannon laughed. "He might as well have."

How does she know? That magpie had clearly been spying on more people than Rowan, but I couldn't afford to let her words sneak into my head and make me doubt myself. "I think you're projecting. You haven't done more than the bare minimum as a council member since your daughter walked out on you."

Aunt Shannon simply smiled. "We'll see."

She and Vanessa walked away, the latter shooting me a smirk over her shoulder, while I stood rigidly on the doorstep. The urge seized me to march to the police station and check to make sure nothing about Harvey's freedom had changed in the past hour, but that would have been rising to her bait.

On the other hand, if she or her familiar *had* somehow gained up-to-date information from my brother, then I wanted to know sooner than later. Before I could question my decision, I was out of the house and walking at top speed towards the high street and the police station.

Tansy ran to catch me up. "Are you sure about this?"

"No, but she's kind of right," I said breathlessly. "I'm not going to be able to focus on my job until I at least try to fix this mess."

Upon reaching the police station, I found the various members of the Sky Hopper team milling around outside, conversing in shocked whispers. Gabriel was notably absent, as was Harvey... and Tomas. *Oh, no. Something new did happen.*

I hurried over to join the team members. "What's going on?"

"You don't know?" Cole studied my face, his brow furrowed in concern. "Harvey is in custody."

My mouth went dry. "He wasn't an hour ago. Why?"

"That's what we're here to find out," Gwen put in. "We're not going to stand for it."

"Exactly," added Everly.

At least Harvey had the rest of the team on his side... or most of them. "Where's Gabriel?"

Gwen scowled. "Hiding, if he has any sense."

Uh-oh. "Why?"

"We just found out that he has a history of cheating at Sky Hopper," said Cole. "Jansen and Harvey picked him for the team anyway and claimed that he'd turned over a new leaf, but not everyone sees it that way."

So they didn't already know? "Tomas knew. That's why he was bullying him."

"Did *you* know?" Gwen eyed me suspiciously.

"Not until today," I admitted. "I found out from... well, from Casey."

"He knew, did he?" Cole's jaw twitched in annoyance. "I bet he's thrilled to see us all in disarray."

"So you didn't all get along with him."

"Are you kidding?" Gwen said. "His attitude was almost as bad as Tomas's is these days. Speaking of whom, Tomas is talking to the police and trying to convince them to let Harvey out, but they aren't buying it."

"Tomas is trying to help him?" I couldn't keep the scepticism out of my tone. "I thought he hated you all."

"No, he hates Gabriel—and now I understand why," Cole replied. "Since he's realised how much trouble Harvey is in though, he must be trying to change their minds."

I had my doubts. Tomas remained at the top of the suspect list as far as I was concerned, but the team had bigger problems now that their captain was in police custody. *I have to help him.*

I walked into the police station and heard Tomas's voice coming from Ramsey's office. My hands curled into fists, but before I could barge in, the door opened, and he came out of the room.

A bolt of anger hit me at the sight of Tomas's scowling face. "They let you go but took Harvey into custody? Seriously?"

"Yes." He tried to sidestep me, but I "accidentally" blocked him with the sceptre. It was at that point that he finally seemed to notice who I was. "What's the problem?"

"I want to talk to you alone. Outside."

He shrugged. "Sure, why not. What's one more inter-rogation?"

If he was trying for sympathy, he was barking up the wrong tree. I ignored his sulky expression as he followed me out of the police station, and I made sure the rest of the team was out of earshot before turning on him. "You don't seem bothered that your captain is in custody."

"I am," he argued. "What I'm not is surprised. Harvey

was keeping so many secrets that it's no wonder they assumed him guilty."

My hands fisted again, and several pigeons flew over to perch on the gutter above our heads. "And you thought now was a good time to tell the entire team about Gabriel's history of cheating?"

"What of it?" he retaliated. "They deserved to know."

"Jansen already knew, but someone killed him," I said. "Is that why you've been acting up at practise sessions? Trying to bully Gabriel into quitting?"

"So what if I have?"

I gave him a challenging stare. "If you want there to still *be* a team by the end of the week, then I'd suggest coming clean about everything *you're* hiding."

"I have no idea what you're talking about."

"Jansen died immediately after hiring Gabriel. Don't you think that's an odd coincidence? Especially as most of the team didn't know?"

"That's *why* I told them, to find out if any of them did." He glowered at me. "What's your point?"

Did he seriously want me to spell out every detail? "I know Harvey, and I also know you were in possession of the badge Jansen choked to death on. It was right in front of you throughout the entire party."

"The badge was the captain's, not mine."

"It was on *your* table," I said pointedly. "If you didn't put it there, who did?"

"You think I killed Jansen."

Finally, the penny drops. "Give me one good reason why I should believe you didn't. The murder weapon was in front of you, you disapproved of his replacement, and you have zero respect for your teammates."

He blew out a breath. "I was nowhere near Jansen at the time, and I can't do magic."

I raised a brow. "At all?"

"No." A blotchy flush spread across his face. "I couldn't have levitated the badge over to him. Happy?"

Not really was the honest answer. But I couldn't think of how he'd managed to sneak that badge into Jansen's cake without magic unless he'd asked someone else to do it for him. Or managed a feat of extreme sleight of hand in front of a crowd. Not impossible, but before I could say another word, he walked away.

Incensed, I marched back towards the police station and nearly collided with Ramsey coming out the doors. "I thought you were going home."

"You seriously took Harvey into custody?"

"You make it sound more serious than it is, Robin."

"It *is* serious," I hissed. "Didn't you at least question Tomas about his own potential involvement? Did you check *his* phone?"

"We did check his messages," Ramsey said. "He didn't send anything the night of the party, not to anyone."

"He was on his phone the whole time. I *saw* him."

"He claimed to be browsing the Wizarding Web, and it looks like that's true."

"What about the badge then?"

"He said the badge wasn't his. Someone else left it on the table."

"Of course he'd say that," I snarled. "He just told the entire team about Gabriel's history of cheating and claimed he did it because he wanted to scare someone into a confession. I think he's just trying to sabotage them again."

"Maybe it's true, but that doesn't make him a murderer."

"What makes you think Harvey is then?"

"I don't think he's a killer, but I also can't make excuses for him, Robin." He spoke gently but firmly, which was worse than an outright accusation. My heart dropped even further when he reached into his pocket and pulled out my camera. "You can have this back now."

"So that's it then." He'd dismissed me altogether, and all I'd managed to do was compile more evidence in Tomas's favour rather than against him.

This can't be it. It can't be over.

14

I paced away from the police station with the camera in my hands, tempted to wipe the memory clean so that at least I didn't have the constant reminders of that awful night on record. If it wasn't any use as evidence, what was the sense of rubbing salt in the wound?

Tansy scampered at my feet. "You know *I* could go and speak to him, don't you?"

"Who?" I glanced down at her. "Tomas?"

"Harvey, of course. I can tell him you tried your best to get him out."

"You don't think my brother would notice my familiar sneaking around the jail? You're the only red squirrel in town."

"And proud of it." She fluffed out her tail. "I can be as sneaky as that magpie when I want to be."

Speaking of magpies, I thought I should probably tell Rowan about her sister's sojourn as a frog. She'd get some amusement out of that, at least. "If you want to talk to him, then feel free."

I was less than convinced that it would change anything at this point, but Tansy must have been back to her usual self if she was in the mood for a stealth mission, and it'd keep her firmly away from my aunt's traps. Tansy scampered away, while I veered towards Were's My Coffee?

Since the café itself was closed for the night, I messaged Rowan, asking her to let me in through the back door. The door opened within a minute, and she beckoned me into the narrow hallway.

"What's up with you? You look like you saw my mother." A pause. "Wait... you didn't, did you?"

"I did, and that's not even the worst of it."

"What could possibly be worse than *her*?" Rowan retreated upstairs. "I was going to call for takeout, but I can go with you to the Fox's Den if you want to talk about it."

"It's up to you. Fair warning—I probably shouldn't stay out too late, or else my mother will think I've been arrested too."

"Too?" She paused with her hand on the door to her flat. "No way. Harvey hasn't been arrested, has he?"

"He's in custody, which is basically the same thing." I exhaled in a sigh and followed her into the room. "I screwed up, Rowan."

"Tell me everything."

I did so while Rowan called for a takeaway pizza delivery. That was more than welcome, since I'd been too frazzled to remember to eat anything when I'd got in from work, and my energy was flagging from all the dashing around I'd been doing. At least eating pizza on the sofa in front of a video game with Rowan would make me feel somewhat normal, though the stabbing guilt at Harvey's predicament refused to abate.

When I'd finished recounting the day's disastrous turn of events to Rowan, she swore under her breath. "Tomas *must* be guilty. It makes no sense for him not to be. The badge was right in front of his nose, right? He didn't even deny it."

"He insists he can't use magic, so he can't have levitated the badge across to the table while we were cutting the cake," I explained. "There are other ways for him to have pulled it off, but my brother is officially done with humouring me. I'm on my own."

"Where's Tansy then?"

"She went to speak to Harvey and get the details from him." I picked up another slice of pizza. "I'd like to know what pushed them into taking him into custody, but I'm guessing it had to do with those messages he sent to Jansen."

"Were they really that incriminating?"

"According to my brother, the messages sounded like Harvey was blackmailing Jansen into staying on the team by denying him the money he was owed." I dropped the pizza slice back onto the plate. "Never mind that Jansen would have bankrupted the team if he'd been allowed to look after the money himself. It doesn't help that Harvey also knew about Gabriel's history of cheating either."

"Gabriel's the new guy, right?" She drew in a breath. "So that's why certain people had an issue with him."

"Yes, and it was Jansen who made the call to let him onto the team anyway. Harvey, too, but I can't see this not being connected to the murder." I wiped pizza grease from my hands on a tissue before getting out my camera and skimming through the photos again. "If I could just pin down where Tomas was standing right before Jansen died, I can figure out how he sneaked the badge across the room without magic."

Most of the photos showed him sulking in the background while the rest of the team posed for the camera, his head hunched over his mobile phone. Since it was impossible to see his screen from this angle, it was tricky to tell if he was messaging someone or just browsing the web. The badge remained consistently on the table in front of him throughout—but I paused on the very last photograph, taken just before the cake had been cut. When I zoomed in on the back table, the badge was no longer there. Neither was Tomas.

I zoomed out again in an attempt to find him, and my gaze snagged on Jansen sitting at the front with the cake knife in his hand. The other players were gathered around him, but while I counted the correct number of team members, Tomas wasn't within sight. Who was the extra player? I counted them again and then zoomed in before panning across each figure.

I came to a halt at a blurred male figure standing behind Jansen. While I couldn't see his face, suspicion gripped me. *He's not a team member.*

A flutter of wings came from the direction of the window, followed by a thud. I put down the camera. "I think someone just flew into your trap."

Rowan jumped to her feet. "At last."

She and I crossed the room to the window, which Rowan unlocked. A very sticky magpie tumbled into the room, covered in webbing. Careful not to entangle my own fingers, I caught her in my hands and lifted her into the air.

"Let me go!" Myrtle screeched. "I can't move my wings!"

"Serves you right for spying on us." I looked up at Rowan. "I forgot to mention what I did to Vanessa earlier, but I bet that's why she's here."

Rowan eyed me. "What *did* you do to Vanessa?"

"She tried to hex me, so I reversed her own spell against her and turned her into a frog."

She snorted. "Is she still hopping around?"

"No, I turned her back before she threw a tantrum."

"Pity."

Myrtle gave another loud screech. "If you don't let me go, I'll have my witch turn this place to dust."

"I'm not letting you go until you promise to stop spying on Rowan."

"Exactly." Rowan glowered down at the magpie in my hands. "Tell my mother that if she wants to talk to me, she can text or call me like a normal parent."

A flash of red, fluffy tail appeared outside the window. Then Tansy vaulted inside, landing on the arm of the sofa. "You caught her? Nice job."

Myrtle flapped her wings, to no effect. "Yes, how very clever of you. Now let me go."

"I don't think so." I held out my hands towards Rowan. "Can you hold her for a second while I talk to Tansy?"

"Sure." Rowan moved in to take the struggling magpie out of my hands, while I went to the opposite side of the room with Tansy so that Myrtle wouldn't hear every word we spoke to one another.

"Did you see Harvey?" I asked Tansy in an undertone.

"Briefly," she replied. "He seems surprised that Tomas told the whole team about Gabriel's cheating."

"Why does he keep going out of his way to defend that guy?" I shook my head. "Didn't he have any theories on who actually did it then?"

"He said the killer's intention was likely to split the team apart. It wasn't necessarily just about Jansen *or* Gabriel. That's why he doesn't think Tomas did it."

Hmm. Tomas might be a nuisance and a bully, but he wasn't likely to gain anything in particular from the entire team going down with the sinking broomstick. If I believed Harvey's faith in him and accepted that his change in behaviour was recent, then who *did* have the most to gain from the team falling to pieces?

Perhaps... someone who'd already left the team behind.

I went over to the sofa, picked up my camera, and showed Tansy the last photo. "Recognise that guy behind Jansen?"

She hopped onto my arm and peered at the picture. "No. Why?"

"He's not part of the team." The image was crowded, too blurred to make out his face, but it was all I needed. "Who exactly confirmed Casey's alibi the night of the party?"

Tansy lifted her head. "You think I know? Ask Ramsey."

"I doubt he's willing to hear another wild theory from my direction."

Hang on. Hadn't Vanessa said she'd been at the Mermaid's Meadow the other night? That they'd held a themed event over the weekend, perhaps the same night as the party? Granted, she was unlikely to want to give me the time of day after the incident earlier, but I was out of any better ideas, and we still had to return the magpie to her owner anyway.

Camera in hand, I returned to Rowan's side. "I have a question for Myrtle."

"What?" The magpie continued to struggle against the sticky webbing. "I won't betray my witch. Never!"

"Calm down. I don't want your family secrets. I want to know if Vanessa went to the Mermaid's Meadow on Friday night."

Myrtle's bulging eyes fixed on me. "Why on earth do you want to know?"

"Just answer the question. It's not a trick. Or remotely relevant to your scheming. Tell me, and I'll let you go."

"You'd better be telling the truth," croaked the magpie. "Yes, she was at the Mermaid's Meadow."

"Excellent." I nodded to Rowan. "I'm taking you back to your witch. With a warning."

"What?" Rowan went pale. "Please tell me you have a plan, Robin."

"I do, but first, we're delivering our little spy back to her owner. Afterwards, I want to talk to your sister."

Her brows shot up. "After you turned her into a frog?"

"She turned herself into a frog. Technicalities." I held out my hands. "Give her here. I'll take her back."

Myrtle cawed loudly, and Rowan let go of her with a hiss of pain when the magpie launched into a lopsided flight. Remnants of the webbing spell clung to her wings, but she flew in a zigzag across the room and out the open window.

"I'll get her." Tansy did a flying leap across the sofa, while Rowan and I hurried out of the flat and downstairs.

By the time we left the alleyway alongside the café, Myrtle had already taken flight. Tansy gave chase across the rooftops, while I faced Rowan. "We both know where she went. I'm going after her."

Rowan hesitated for an instant. "I'll come with you."

"No… you don't have to. Not unless you're sure."

She dropped her gaze. "I've been having nightmares about that awful house ever since I left. It's kind of pathetic, but I feel like sneaking out the back door meant I never really had closure. I never faced up to them. So… now's my chance."

"Are you sure you're ready though?"

"No, but I'll never know unless I try." She nodded to me. "Let's move."

We made our way down the high street, following my familiar's lead. Rowan walked alongside me, her face set, but despite her fierce determination, I could tell what it cost her to go back to her family home after finally breaking free. Yet she'd agreed to do it anyway, and while she had her own reasons for wanting closure, it'd been her desire to help me that had finally pushed her over the edge.

Given that I'd already antagonised Vanessa and her mother within the past few hours, I expected nothing short of belligerence to await us at my aunt's house, so I figured we might as well go in with all guns blazing. We kept our wands at the ready—or the sceptre in my case— and I held it upright in my free hand when I rang the doorbell to Aunt Shannon's house.

The door sprang open. Aunt Shannon filled the entryway, her familiar perched on her shoulder and not a single piece of webbing to be seen. "Do you think you're amusing?"

Ignoring her question, I deliberately echoed her own words from earlier. "I'd like to talk to your daughter."

"My daughter is recovering from what you put her through earlier." Then she spotted my companion, and her eyes bulged. "What is that awful colour?"

Of all the things to comment on, Rowan's freshly dyed pink hair wasn't at the top of my list, but Aunt Shannon's stunned expression betrayed her genuine shock that her youngest daughter had dared to show her face here.

"She has better taste than you do," I told her. "Also, I didn't put Vanessa through anything but her own hex, so she'll live. Anyway, I happen to need her help with a murder investigation."

Aunt Shannon's shock became incredulity. "First you attack my familiar, now you have the gall to demand my daughter's help?"

"Your familiar flew into my window while trying to spy on me," Rowan spoke up. "You ought to know about taking precautions to keep unwanted animals from getting into your house."

Ha. Aunt Shannon said nothing for an instant, while Vanessa's voice came from the hallway behind her. "What's *she* doing here?"

"There you are." I addressed Vanessa over Aunt Shannon's shoulder. "Vanessa, you were at the Mermaid's Meadow on Friday night, weren't you?"

"What?" She scoffed. "Yes, I was. Why do you want to know?"

"Was there a man working at the bar who was wearing the uniform of the local Sky Hopper team?"

"What?" she said blankly. "What on earth do you want to know that for?"

"One of the staff members at the Mermaid's Meadow is a murder suspect." I figured the truth would invite the fewest irrelevant questions. "It's a simple yes-or-no answer. Did you see anyone wearing that uniform?"

"Is this about your boyfriend's murder accusation?"

My jaw twitched. "Just answer the question."

Apparently, something in my expression convinced her. "Yeah, I saw someone in the uniform. Figured it was a fancy-dress costume."

That was enough for me. "That's all we needed to know."

I turned away, while Rowan took a brief step forward. "Also, Mother, do me a favour and keep your familiar away from my home."

And with that, we left the two of them staring after us in bewilderment. While I kept my sceptre at the ready, neither of them retaliated, though I could have sworn Rowan didn't breathe out until we reached the end of the road.

"That was... terrifying." She exhaled shakily. "But I'm glad I did it."

"You did great," I told her. "And we got what we needed. Not a definite confirmation, but I think my hunch is right."

"I'm still lost, to be honest," she said. "That Casey... he was the guy who left the team? Was he at the party?"

"He works at the Mermaid's Meadow and claimed he was there while everyone was at the party," I explained.

"It's possible he sneaked into the party dressed in his old uniform and then slipped out again before the police showed up. There were so many people in costume that it wouldn't have registered, but if Vanessa saw someone dressed in the uniform at the nightclub, then they couldn't have been among the suspects."

Her eyes rounded. "You're going to speak to him now then?"

"If you see Ramsey, can you let him know where I am?" When she gave me a doubtful look, I added, "I don't have long. He might already know I'm onto him."

Given that the whole team knew about Gabriel's cheating by now, someone else might come to the same conclusion I had. Casey might have feigned ignorance earlier, but his reaction to Gabriel joining the team had rung true. And he'd skipped over giving a clear reason why *he'd* left the team.

This time, I wouldn't let him dodge the question.

15

I walked at speed towards the Mermaid's Meadow, hoping I wasn't already too late. While confronting Casey without backup aside from my familiar wasn't the wisest of plans, Rowan had done enough on my account already in going back to her awful relatives to help me out. As for Ramsey… he was many things, but he wasn't a fighter, and he was also hamstrung by having to keep an eye on all his suspects.

Which included everyone except the actual culprit. If I was right, that is, but I couldn't afford to second-guess myself at this point.

While I walked at a fast pace, I couldn't shake the feeling that I'd already missed my chance to apprehend the killer in all the time I'd wasted chasing false leads. There was no point in lamenting lost time though, so I kept a firm grip on the sceptre until I reached the Mermaid's Meadow.

"Want to come in?" I whispered to Tansy.

She hopped onto my shoulder. "Let's get him."

Nudging the door inward, I stepped out onto the sticky floor and began to make my way across the room. An unfamiliar witch was working at the bar this time around, and her mouth fell open at the sight of the sceptre in my hand.

"Hey, there," I said to her. "Is Casey still around?"

"He's in the back," she replied. "I'll get him."

"I need to talk to him in private," I explained. "It's urgent."

The witch backed through a door and called out, "Casey!"

No response came. My hand clenched on the sceptre. Had he done a runner? There were several people already in the bar, so he might have wanted to avoid a public stir, but if he'd got wind of Gabriel's cheating past being exposed to the whole team, it was more likely that he'd taken off altogether.

The witch returned to the bar. "I can't find him. He's gonna get fired if he keeps skiving off in the middle of his shifts."

"Did he do the same on Friday evening, by any chance?"

She blinked at me. "How'd you know? He was gone nearly an hour. We had to call someone in to take over from him, and then he wasn't even in his work uniform when he came back."

That settles that then. "Thanks anyway."

I retreated to the door, Tansy clinging to my shoulder, and found no signs of Casey outside. If he'd sneaked out the back, then I might already be too late to catch up to him, but I refused to let Harvey languish in jail in his place.

"I'll get him." Tansy leapt from my shoulder to the fence that ran alongside the building, landing in the alleyway on the other side. I kept a tight grip on my sceptre as I one-handedly clambered over the fence myself, to be greeted with a yell of surprise when I landed on top of Casey.

"Gotcha."

"What's your problem?" Casey jerked out from underneath me before I could grab him.

I raised the sceptre and pointed the end directly at him. "Have fun at the party on Friday night? I'm surprised you kept your old team uniform if you hated them so much, but I guess it would come in handy if you wanted to blend into a crowd at one of their parties."

Casey was silent for a moment, and I could practically see the thoughts spinning in his skull, hunting for a way out. "What are you talking about?"

"You need to work on your alibis, Casey. Your coworkers aren't that impressed with you for disappearing twice in a week."

His hand twitched towards his pocket, but Tansy jumped on his wrist and bit him before he could grab his wand. He shook her off with a hiss of pain. "I wouldn't do anything rash, Head Witch."

"What, like murdering your former captain?"

How could I have overlooked him as a suspect? I'd been too fixated on the current team members to even consider someone who'd already left them behind, but the same could have been said for the police. Everyone had taken his alibi as sufficient, to the extent that he'd walked straight back into his place of employment in his old uniform and hardly raised an eyebrow.

Never mind being fired… the guy needed to be arrested. He'd killed someone and would have happily let an innocent man take the blame for his crimes just so he could destroy the team that he'd left behind. Gabriel being chosen must have been the last straw for him.

I took aim with the sceptre, but he jerked to the side and lifted his wand, pointing it over my shoulder. His own spell hit the fence, sending us both crashing into a heap of splintered wood. With reflexes no doubt honed by his years on the Sky Hopper team, he rolled to his feet and broke into a run.

With the sceptre in my grip, I was slower to disentangle myself from the mess of wooden fence panels, but Tansy launched into a sprint so fast she turned into a blur. As she sailed towards Casey, he swung his leg over a broomstick he must have grabbed from the back of the nightclub.

Oh, damn. He kept his old broom there as well.

I caught up to Tansy in time to see Casey's figure disappearing into the sky. She scaled the nearest wall, balancing on her hind legs, but Casey was far out of reach.

"You don't have wings, Tansy," I called up to her. "And *I* don't have a broomstick stashed anywhere around here."

She jumped down to a lower level. "Use the sceptre, Robin."

"I'm pretty sure it won't let me use it as a mount."

Even my sceptre was no substitute for a broomstick. Running home to grab my broom would take too long, and conjuring spells had never been my strong suit. They took too long to set up, besides…

Wait. Grandma's lessons with the sceptre had mostly revolved around her ordering me to use magnified versions of simple spells, but at one point, she'd definitely mentioned being able to bypass the usual limitations of more complex spells.

Did the same apply to conjuring spells? One way to find out. I waved the sceptre, picturing my own broomstick in my mind's eye—and a split-second's rushing sound was my only warning before the end of the broom hit me in the face.

"Ow. Stop laughing at me, Tansy."

"You did it though!" She hopped onto my shoulder, while I swung a leg over the broomstick. "Don't drop that sceptre."

"Wasn't planning to."

I took flight in a single bound, one eye on the rapidly shrinking form of Casey in the overcast sky. He could fly incredibly well, which was to be expected of a former Sky Hopper player, and no doubt he'd kept his fancy broomstick when he'd quit. Mine was a bog-standard edition several years out of date, while my decent-at-best flight skills weren't enough to compete with those of a seasoned player. The sceptre weighing down my hand and causing my flight path to veer slightly to the left didn't help much either.

On the other hand, we weren't in a game. Using magic against the other players was a big no-no in professional matches, but to catch a killer, I'd use all of the available skills in my arsenal.

I picked up speed, pushing my broomstick to its limits until the wood creaked. The breeze, which hadn't been noticeable back on the ground, battered me in the face, and Tansy had to dig her claws into my shoulder to keep from being swept away.

"Hang on tight," I told her. "I'll have to stop that broom of his."

Preferably without him falling to his death before the police could get a proper confession out of him. I held on one-handed and aimed the sceptre at his back, but my first spell flew wide by a mile.

"I need him to slow down before I can cast a slowing spell," I remarked to Tansy. "Yeah, that's not gonna work."

"You don't have to use the sceptre," Tansy said in my ear. "Play to your strengths, remember?"

"My strengths?" What did she mean by that? I'd left my camera at Rowan's, and while the sceptre was certainly powerful, it was wildly uncontrollable by nature.

I aimed the sceptre at his back again. A nearby seagull squawked in displeasure as my spell clipped its wing. *Wait.*

Of course I had one last trick up my sleeve. Raising my voice, I called on all the birds in the region who could possibly hear my shout.

"Get that broomstick!" I shouted. "Drag him out of the sky!"

My shout was loud enough for even Casey himself to hear, judging by the brief glance he cast over his shoulder, though I was too far behind to see his expression. More's the pity, because I would have liked to snap a picture of his face when the first group of pigeons descended upon him.

As he swatted the pigeons away with a hand, another flock rose from the forest below to converge on his broom. He'd chosen a route above the Wildwood, away from any human witnesses, but there were a lot of nonhuman ears listening in the forest below, and when I called, they answered in a chorus.

Casey gave a frustrated yell when a pigeon flew into his arm and knocked his wand out of his hand. Tansy laughed with delight, while I found myself gaining on him with every passing second as he was forced to slow down to deflect a never-ending stream of birds.

I caught up to him as he let out another shout of anger, his broomstick bucking under the sudden influx of birds. They ranged from sparrows to blackbirds, crows to magpies, even an owl or two who'd been woken from their sleep by the range of my voice. Their collective weight pressed his broom downwards until I got close enough to address the whole flock.

"Fly him back to Wildwood Heath," I told them. "Try not to drop him."

"Let me go!" he yelled, his voice muffled by the deluge of feathers.

More birds continued to join the fray, while Casey struggled to regain control over his broomstick. He was fighting a losing battle, however. The birds collectively turned him around, pointing towards Wildwood Heath. While they propelled his broomstick over the forests and fields, I flew at his side, enjoying the entertainment as he struggled to shake off the feathery horde.

When we overlooked the town, I gave a final order: "Drop him off at the police station. Make sure he doesn't run."

The flock of birds carried Casey downwards over the rooftops, and the townspeople raised their heads to gape in surprise as we flew down in front of the police station.

The instant Casey's broomstick touched the ground, a

swathe of birds ripped it from his hands, while more of them pinned him to the ground. The last bird to land on his head was a robin. Perhaps not as appropriate as a dodo, but I appreciated a little poetic justice when I saw it. *Got him.*

16

Once they'd deposited their quarry, the birds took flight in a shower of feathers and droppings. Unfortunately for everyone standing outside the police station, the latter mostly landed on their heads. Including Tomas, to my amusement. He might have been innocent of murder, but he was still an unpleasant person who'd caused his team no end of grief, so I didn't care if he ended up covered in bird droppings.

In the ensuing chaos, Casey tried to make a run for it. Ready for him, I aimed the sceptre at his back, but it was hard to avoid hitting anyone else with the growing crowd assembling outside the police station.

Tansy jumped on his face, her fluffy tail blocking him from seeing where he was going, while I addressed the other team members. "He's the one who killed Jansen. Can you help me get him into the police station?"

To my relief, they acted fast enough once they figured out what was happening. By the time we'd dragged him through the automatic doors, everyone in the police station had already come into the lobby to find out why there were a hundred birds making a racket outside. Ramsey strode to the front, looking around in confusion at the team members shedding feathers all over the floor. "What is going on out there?"

"This is Casey, the murderer." I jabbed him in the back with my sceptre. "He tried to fly away, so I had to improvise to catch him. His wand is lost in the Wildwood somewhere, but I'd lock his broom away as soon as possible if I were you."

Ramsey's confusion disappeared, and his expression settled into the steeliness of the police captain looking down at an incoming criminal. "Is he willing to confess?"

Casey said nothing. His gaze darted around, but a wall of Sky Hopper players kept him from retreating out the doors, and the rest of the police officers filled the remaining space in the lobby. He was trapped, and he knew it.

"Take him to the cells," Ramsey told the surrounding officers.

Casey swore. "So what if I killed the old man? He pressured me into quitting the team after I called him out on his spending habits, and yet he hired that cheater without a second's thought."

So that was the real story. Once again, I gave myself a mental kick for not realising the obvious sooner, but from the tightening expression on Ramsey's face, he'd had the same realisation himself.

As for the rest of the team, their expressions ranged from stunned to enraged.

"You're despicable," Gwen told him.

"Agreed." Cole gave Ramsey a pointed look. "Right, you're going to let Harvey go now, aren't you?"

"Yeah, let him out," one of the others said.

Everyone else chimed in with agreement, and my heart lifted to see their show of support for their captain. Even Tomas, though he gave me a dirty look when he caught my glance in his direction. I shot him a grin in return, unable to spare any annoyance for him. Casey was on his way to a cell, and Harvey would walk free.

"Take him away," Ramsey said to the officers who surrounded Casey. "And bring Harvey Walton out here."

I expected Casey to make another last-ditch escape attempt, but he didn't fight when the police hauled him away. The team's boos followed him across the lobby and through a door at the back, while the police officers began to disperse in all directions.

Ramsey tutted, eyeing the feathers strewn all over the lobby. "Someone has to tidy this up. Couldn't you have picked a less... *messy* way to bring him into custody, Robin?"

"I couldn't catch him on a broom, so this was my last option," I protested. "He's a professional flier, remember?"

Unconvinced, Ramsey's gaze skimmed over the bird-dropping-covered players. "Is the outside of the building in the same state?"

Worse, probably, was the honest answer, but I couldn't have cared less about the mess the birds had left behind. Neither could anyone else. Only Tomas looked less than thrilled, though that might have been because he couldn't get the bird droppings out of his hair. Too bad for him.

The lobby fell silent when Harvey walked out of the back room. He stopped dead when he came into view of his team members—and me—and his shock melted into relief.

"They're letting me go?"

"Yes." Cole punched the air in triumph. Two of the team members high-fived, and another instigated a team hug which ended with Harvey covered in feathers and bird droppings too.

"What is all this?" Harvey picked a feather out of his hair, bemused. "Did I hear right? Casey... *he* killed Jansen?"

"He did," I confirmed. "He almost got away, but I chased him down and sent a flock of birds to drag him back to town. Hence the feathers."

"You..." He trailed off, stunned, and then shook his head at his teammates. "You're all here. Why?"

"Initially, because Tomas was a tattletale and decided to stir up trouble," Gwen replied. "But then we stayed to make sure you walked free."

Tomas scoffed. "I only told everyone the truth because I knew the killer must know Gabriel's history, so I wanted to figure out who else did. When it turned out nobody else on the team knew except for me..."

"I knew it was Casey," I ventured. "Though you didn't make yourself look innocent in the slightest, Tomas. Why *did* you have that badge on the table?"

"I told you, it wasn't mine. I think it was Jansen's, actually."

Casey must have grabbed it on his way across the room. The guy couldn't rot in a cell for long enough, as far as I was concerned.

Harvey cleared his throat. "Regardless, if everyone on the team is aware of the facts, then I think it's appropriate for us to discuss Gabriel's past as a group. Is that all right?"

Murmurs travelled among the group, while the general air of euphoria dimmed a little.

"Gabriel started playing Sky Hopper professionally as a teenager," he began. "A while ago, he was found to have cheated in a match by using a spell not permitted in the rulebook. He received a warning for that incident and was banned from playing for a year, but I knew his history when he came forwards to try out as Jansen's replacement. As I believe in second chances, I decided to let him."

At that, he paused as if to allow the others to voice any objections. Nobody did so, though Tomas wore his customary scowl, his arms folded and his shoulders hunched.

"Out of everyone in the trials, Gabriel was a clear standout," Harvey said. "He didn't cheat, and he certainly didn't do anything to make me believe he wasn't a good fit for the team. I can understand why some of you would have reservations if you became aware of his history, and I am sorry I didn't bring up the matter with all of you before I made the decision. Jansen would agree."

Everyone was quiet for a moment. Then Cole said, "We've all made mistakes at some time or other. I say we let him stay."

"Agreed," said Everly. "He played best in the tryouts, and why scupper our chances? He's already apologised."

Murmurs of agreement ensued. Gwen remained displeased, but she begrudgingly caved when one of the other team members admitted to doing something similar to Gabriel in a game at the academy.

"I've seen worse in professional matches," she grunted.

"I'll give him another chance, as long as he doesn't screw this up."

Tomas scowled. "I don't like him. Or trust him, either."

Harvey faced him. "You're entitled to your opinion, but I would prefer it if you conducted yourself in an appropriate manner in team practise sessions. If Gabriel stays on the team, then he's your fellow player, and you're to treat him as such. Otherwise, you'll find yourself with a warning of your own."

Tomas grunted. "Right, Captain."

"If you'd rather leave, then feel free," added Gwen. "Simple enough."

"I'm not leaving." He lifted his chin in defiance. "We can start from scratch at the next practise session."

"Exactly," Harvey said. "Like I said, I believe in second chances. Is everyone ready to try again?"

Several enthusiastic yeses followed, and the mood rose once again as the truth sank in. Their captain was free, while the rest of the team would be able to continue practising without any further interrogations from the police. Meanwhile, if Tomas made trouble for anyone without cause, he wouldn't get any leniency.

"All right," Harvey said. "Go home and change, and then come and meet me at the Fox's Den in an hour. Deal?"

More cheering followed, and the team began to depart through the automatic doors, shedding feathers as they did so. Only Harvey remained behind, which confused me for a moment until I remembered that the police still had his phone in their possession.

Catching my eye, Ramsey addressed Harvey. "I'll get your possessions back to you right away."

The instant he'd vanished, Harvey and I looked at one another for a long minute before breaking into identical grins.

"You did all this?" He indicated the mass of feathers carpeting the ground outside the automatic doors, where Tansy was having the time of her life, chasing the unlucky stragglers from among the birds who'd brought Casey's broom down.

"I guess I did," I answered.

He gave a laugh. "I don't believe they let me go."

"Me neither, but the killer is in custody, so they had no reason to keep you there. Plus, you know, you're innocent."

"There is that," he said. "Coming to the Fox's Den?"

"Absolutely." A rush of giddy happiness came over me, and I threw my arms around him. Without conscious thought, I found myself kissing him. He made a noise of surprise before responding with enthusiasm—at least until my brother returned and cleared his throat loudly.

"I believe this is yours." Ramsey more or less threw Harvey's mobile phone in his general direction, which he caught one-handed before we broke apart, laughing, and then ran for the door.

"Now I'm covered in feathers too." I sidestepped Tansy, who was engaged in a neck-and-neck chase with a pigeon. "I'd better go home and change."

It wasn't *exactly* the romantic first kiss I'd imagined, but then again, nothing about our relationship was going to be ordinary. Since I'd managed to get him out of being arrested though, I could deal with anything else certain family members of mine threw in our way.

———

"So I hear you apprehended a criminal yesterday." Grandma's greeting when she reappeared in my office was delivered in a matter-of-fact tone, as if she'd utterly forgotten our clashes earlier that week.

"Who told you?" Either Mum or Carmilla, I assumed. "Never mind."

"Never mind?" she repeated. "I hope you used the sceptre."

"I'd have used the sceptre on him, but he was flying at top speed." When she gave me a sceptical look, I added, "I wanted to arrest him, not cause him to fall to his death. I don't know if you've ever used the sceptre from the back of a broomstick, but it's hard enough to cast spells using a regular wand from that angle."

"What in the world did you do then?"

Since when was she remotely interested? It wasn't as if *I'd* been the killer's target this time around, and she'd displayed zero interest in talking about the investigation up until now.

"I convinced a flock of birds to drag him back to town by force."

"Did you now?" She cackled so loudly that Chloe jumped in her seat, while Carmilla woke up from her nap with a disgruntled meow. "Excellent. I wish I'd seen."

From Grandma, that was high praise—and unexpected. "I can try the same again the next time someone tries to assassinate me."

"Oh, no," she said. "No, you must learn to use that sceptre of yours. In fact, I think it's imperative that we learn more about it as soon as possible."

"You mean the sceptre you carried around for decades?" I raised a brow. "Don't you already know it inside out?"

"I thought I did until you came along and claimed it for your own," she said. "Or should I say, it claimed you. It's rare for a sceptre to pick someone without any experience in the role, but its reasons needn't be so opaque."

"You really don't have to rub it in, you know, Grandma."

Carmilla yawned. "She's not insulting you. She's pointing out that you've been selected as a pawn by a powerful magical object and that we ought to take it seriously."

"A pawn?" I echoed. "Yeah, no thanks. I find it hard to believe that nobody knows anything about why the sceptres act the way they do."

"That," said Grandma, "is precisely why we should research the subject ourselves. Or rather, *you* should research it, since I'm unfortunately tethered to this part of town."

"Are you?"

Most spirits were confined to a small area, but Grandma had resolutely refused to admit to her limits up until now. I'd figured it'd take a while for her to adjust to her incorporeal state, and besides, it wasn't as if I'd had any reason to want her to follow me around even more than she already did.

"There's no reason to sound so incredulous." Grandma sniffed. "You and I have a great deal of discussions to have, Robin, and if you're going to insist upon going wherever you like—"

A brief knock on the door interrupted her in mid-sentence. Mum entered the office without waiting for me to invite her in first, but I was glad enough of her cutting off Grandma's lecture to let that one slide.

"Can I help you with something?" I asked her.

Mum looked at me. "Has my mother told you yet?"

"Told me what?" I glanced at Grandma's ghost. "She just mentioned that she doesn't know as much about the sceptre as she thought, since its reasons for picking me as its wielder are so perplexing. Also, she used the word 'pawn,' which I don't appreciate."

"That's not exactly it," Mum said. "But we *do* need to know why the sceptre picked you as its owner, and I believe that information is out there."

"What, on the Wizarding Web?" What had brought this on?

"No, in a library," Mum answered.

My family had officially lost it. "What library? The local one?"

"Regrettably not, but I recently had an enlightening call from the owners of a library in a magical community on the coast," Mum said. "I thought we could make a stop there on the way."

"On the way to where, exactly?" Since when was she planning a holiday? "I thought… wait. Didn't we nominate Wildwood Heath as the location for me to meet the other Head Witches?"

I should have seen that one coming. The instant my life calmed down enough for me to take a breath, the subject of my inevitable meeting with my fellow Head Witches was waiting to pounce on me like a cat on a passing sparrow.

"We did," Mum confirmed. "However, I think it would

be a good idea for you to meet some of them in a less formal setting first."

I drew in a breath. "So it's time then."

"If you're ready."

My mouth opened. I hadn't considered that my mother might be waiting for *me* to be ready, considering that was the opposite of her usual approach of making decisions without my knowledge.

"I… I honestly don't know," I admitted. "I mean, I'm used to meeting with the council by now…"

"This will be the same, but with witches from all over the country," said Mum. "Other than that, there's very little more we can do to prepare you. Most Head Witches learn through practise."

Did that mean she had faith in me to do the same as any other Head Witch? The notion warmed me, I had to admit, though part of me was still wary of these powerful and enigmatic fellow witches who'd been selected as the best of their region.

"If I say yes, am I signing up to do nothing but attend meetings from here on out?"

"Not at all," Mum replied. "You'll still be needed here."

"Good." I'd just started to get used to living in Wildwood Heath again. Not to mention that Harvey wouldn't appreciate it if I ran off.

Part of me was braced for Mum to put her foot down when she found we'd taken the decisive step towards a relationship, if yesterday's public display hadn't already made it clear enough. Ramsey had yet to bring up the subject, though we hadn't had the chance to speak today yet. He'd been too busy trialling Casey for murder and cleaning up the aftermath of the birds' arrival outside the police station. Tansy was still having the best week of her life chasing them around.

Alarm squeezed my chest at the thought of having to abruptly pack my bags and leave. It wasn't a reaction I was used to, considering that I'd pretty much done exactly that the last time I'd moved out of town… but what Harvey and I had was new and fragile enough that I was reluctant to risk severing the thread.

As if she'd picked up on my thoughts, Mum gave me one of her sternest looks. "You can do as you wish in your free time, but when you're with the other Head Witches, you must act like one of them. If not, then some of them will do their best to unseat you, and they won't hesitate to pick up on any weaknesses."

"Like the Henbane Coven," I surmised.

"Worse."

"You're really selling this to me."

"Did you not hear your mother?" said Carmilla. "She's giving you permission to spend your free time at that ridiculous coffee shop and the pub and watching Sky Hopper games."

I raised a brow. "Does that mean you aren't going to argue with me every time I want to meet with Piper?"

"Of course not."

"And Harvey?"

A moment's pause. "No. But be careful to consider how the press might look at the Head Witch's romantic choices. You saw how they treated your father."

It was possibly the first time since their relationship had ended that she'd acknowledged that he'd come off worse from the experience. The press had left Wildwood Heath alone since I'd last driven them out of town, but I was willing to bet they'd be all too happy to make their presence known as soon as I began to travel to meet with other Head Witches.

On the other hand, my family, it seemed, weren't going to stand in my way after all. If playing the Head Witch role was what it took to pursue a relationship with Harvey, so be it. I had no doubt it'd be worth all the fuss.

"I'm well aware of the press," I informed her. "I think Harvey can handle them."

"Who exactly is this Harvey person?" asked Grandma.

"He's the captain of the local Sky Hopper team."

"And he nearly got arrested this week," Carmilla added.

I scowled. "On a false accusation. Ramsey knows we're together."

"You're *what?*" Grandma said.

"Together, Grandma," I said. "Romantically. If anyone has a problem with that, then I'm not taking complaints."

Grandma huffed, while Carmilla gave a coughing laugh. Mum wore her most long-suffering expression, but she said, "As long as you do your job."

"Don't worry. I will."

I got back to work, already counting down the hours until I would go to meet Harvey for a proper date. It was a better reason to keep an eye on the clock than any of my previous ones, I wouldn't lie, and I was glad to get at least one normal date before my career as Head Witch entered its next phase.

Whatever came next, I'd be ready.

ABOUT THE AUTHOR

Elle Adams lives in the middle of England, where she spends most of her time reading an ever-growing mountain of books, planning her next adventure, or writing. Elle's books are humorous mysteries with a paranormal twist, packed with magical mayhem.

She also writes urban and contemporary fantasy novels as Emma L. Adams.

Visit http://www.elleadamsauthor.com/ to find out more about Elle's books.